TO JUDGE THEM

A LAKE DISTRICT THRILLER

DI SAM COBBS 14

M A COMLEY

Copyright © 2024 by M A Comley

All rights reserved.

No part of this book may be reproduced in any form or by any electronic or mechanical means, including information storage and retrieval systems, without written permission from the author, except for the use of brief quotations in a book review.

Thank you once again to Clive Rowlandson for allowing me to use one of his stunning photos for the cover.

ALSO BY M A COMLEY

Blind Justice (Novella)

Cruel Justice (Book #1)

Mortal Justice (Novella)

Impeding Justice (Book #2)

Final Justice (Book #3)

Foul Justice (Book #4)

Guaranteed Justice (Book #5)

Ultimate Justice (Book #6)

Virtual Justice (Book #7)

Hostile Justice (Book #8)

Tortured Justice (Book #9)

Rough Justice (Book #10)

Dubious Justice (Book #11)

Calculated Justice (Book #12)

Twisted Justice (Book #13)

Justice at Christmas (Short Story)

Prime Justice (Book #14)

Heroic Justice (Book #15)

Shameful Justice (Book #16)

Immoral Justice (Book #17)

Toxic Justice (Book #18)

Overdue Justice (Book #19)

Unfair Justice (a 10,000 word short story)

Irrational Justice (a 10,000 word short story)

Seeking Justice (a 15,000 word novella)

Caring For Justice (a 24,000 word novella)
Savage Justice (a 17,000 word novella)
Justice at Christmas #2 (a 15,000 word novella)
Gone in Seconds (Justice Again series #1)
Ultimate Dilemma (Justice Again series #2)
Shot of Silence (Justice Again series #3)
Taste of Fury (Justice Again series #4)
Crying Shame (Justice Again series #5)
See No Evil (Justice Again #6)
To Die For (DI Sam Cobbs #1)
To Silence Them (DI Sam Cobbs #2)
To Make Them Pay (DI Sam Cobbs #3)
To Prove Fatal (DI Sam Cobbs #4)
To Condemn Them (DI Sam Cobbs #5)
To Punish Them (DI Sam Cobbs #6)
To Entice Them (DI Sam Cobbs #7)
To Control Them (DI Sam Cobbs #8)
To Endanger Lives (DI Sam Cobbs #9)
To Hold Responsible (DI Sam Cobbs #10)
To Catch a Killer (DI Sam Cobbs #11)
To Believe The Truth (DI Sam Cobbs #12)
To Blame Them (DI Sam Cobbs #13)
To Judge Them (DI Sam Cobbs #14)
To Fear Him (DI Sam Cobbs #15)
Forever Watching You (DI Miranda Carr thriller)
Wrong Place (DI Sally Parker thriller #1)
No Hiding Place (DI Sally Parker thriller #2)
Cold Case (DI Sally Parker thriller#3)

Deadly Encounter (DI Sally Parker thriller #4)
Lost Innocence (DI Sally Parker thriller #5)
Goodbye My Precious Child (DI Sally Parker #6)
The Missing Wife (DI Sally Parker #7)
Truth or Dare (DI Sally Parker #8)
Where Did She Go? (DI Sally Parker #9)
Sinner (DI Sally Parker #10)
The Good Die Young (DI Sally Parker #11)
Coping Without You (DI Sally Parker #12)
Could It Be Him? (DI Sally Parker #13)
Frozen In Time (DI Sally Parker #14)
Web of Deceit (DI Sally Parker Novella)
The Missing Children (DI Kayli Bright #1)
Killer On The Run (DI Kayli Bright #2)
Hidden Agenda (DI Kayli Bright #3)
Murderous Betrayal (Kayli Bright #4)
Dying Breath (Kayli Bright #5)
Taken (DI Kayli Bright #6)
The Hostage Takers (DI Kayli Bright Novella)
No Right to Kill (DI Sara Ramsey #1)
Killer Blow (DI Sara Ramsey #2)
The Dead Can't Speak (DI Sara Ramsey #3)
Deluded (DI Sara Ramsey #4)
The Murder Pact (DI Sara Ramsey #5)
Twisted Revenge (DI Sara Ramsey #6)
The Lies She Told (DI Sara Ramsey #7)
For The Love Of… (DI Sara Ramsey #8)
Run for Your Life (DI Sara Ramsey #9)

Cold Mercy (DI Sara Ramsey #10)

Sign of Evil (DI Sara Ramsey #11)

Indefensible (DI Sara Ramsey #12)

Locked Away (DI Sara Ramsey #13)

I Can See You (DI Sara Ramsey #14)

The Kill List (DI Sara Ramsey #15)

Crossing The Line (DI Sara Ramsey #16)

Time to Kill (DI Sara Ramsey #17)

Deadly Passion (DI Sara Ramsey #18)

Son Of The Dead (DI Sara Ramsey #19)

Evil Intent (DI Sara Ramsey #20)

The Games People Play (DI Sara Ramsey #21)

Revenge Streak (DI Sara Ramsey #22)

Seeking Retribution (DI Sara Ramsey #23)

Gone… But Where? (DI Sara Ramsey #24)

Last Man Standing (DI Sara Ramsey #25)

I Know The Truth (A Psychological thriller)

She's Gone (A psychological thriller)

Shattered Lives (A psychological thriller)

Evil In Disguise – a novel based on True events

Deadly Act (Hero series novella)

Torn Apart (Hero series #1)

End Result (Hero series #2)

In Plain Sight (Hero Series #3)

Double Jeopardy (Hero Series #4)

Criminal Actions (Hero Series #5)

Regrets Mean Nothing (Hero series #6)

Prowlers (Hero Series #7)

Sole Intention (Intention series #1)

Grave Intention (Intention series #2)

Devious Intention (Intention #3)

Cozy mysteries

Murder at the Wedding

Murder at the Hotel

Murder by the Sea

Death on the Coast

Death By Association

Merry Widow (A Lorne Simpkins short story)

It's A Dog's Life (A Lorne Simpkins short story)

A Time To Heal (A Sweet Romance)

A Time For Change (A Sweet Romance)

High Spirits

The Temptation series (Romantic Suspense/New Adult Novellas)

Past Temptation

Lost Temptation

Clever Deception (co-written by Linda S Prather)

Tragic Deception (co-written by Linda S Prather)

Sinful Deception (co-written by Linda S Prather)

ACKNOWLEDGMENTS

Special thanks as always go to @studioenp for their superb cover design expertise.

My heartfelt thanks go to my wonderful editor Emmy, and my proofreaders Joseph and Barbara for spotting all the lingering nits.

Thank you also to my amazing ARC Group who help to keep me sane during this process.

Mum, you've taken a huge part of my heart with you. A year on and some days are definitely more difficult than others.

To Mary, gone, but never forgotten. I hope you found the peace you were searching for my dear friend. I miss you each and every day.

PROLOGUE

The rain was teeming down. Detective Inspector Sam Cobbs and her partner, Detective Sergeant Bob Jones, had just left the final witness' house and were on their way back to the station in Workington.

"It's extremely satisfying, tying up the loose ends to a case, don't you agree?" she asked.

"I can think of better ways of spending my day rather than setting off in the middle of a torrential storm, just to ensure 'all the ends are tied', whether they are of the loose variety or otherwise. Why is it you never suggest us doing this on a hot, sunny day?"

"Wind your neck in, partner. Let's face it, you wouldn't be you, if you didn't have something to whinge about," she ribbed. She was lucky in that respect; he rarely, if ever, complained, a rarity as partners go, according to some of her colleagues.

"You're going to live to regret saying that, mark my words."

They both laughed because Sam knew he was right. By the time they had reached the station, her eyes were sore from trying to see through the constant rain belting her windscreen and having to deal with the wipers acting as though they were on speed.

"We're going to have to make a run for it."

"What the…? I can't believe you parked in your allotted space and didn't go out of your way to drop me off at the main entrance."

"Hey, pal, if I'm forced to suffer the consequences, then so should you. Sharing is caring and all that."

"Jeez, if you say so. I have another saying… but I don't think it could be classed as appropriate for a lady's ears—that is, if you know one."

Sam dug him in the ribs and then prepared herself to run the forty feet needed to get them in the dry again. "Are you ready?"

Bob had slipped off his jacket and placed it over his head.

Sam copied him, bashing her elbows on the steering wheel a few times in the process. "Ouch, damn, when am I going to learn to keep an umbrella on the back seat?"

"We live and learn, don't we?" Bob hopped out of the car.

She followed seconds later and pressed the key fob to lock the car during her sprint to the main door.

It wasn't until she stopped running and cursing under her breath that she realised her phone was ringing in her jacket pocket. "Damn, it will have to wait."

Bob held the door open for her. The rain lashed against the backs of her legs as he blocked her way with his broad frame.

"Quick, move back. Get out of my way, you big oaf."

"I believe 'thank you' are the words you were searching for," he mumbled.

She rolled her eyes and fought with the soaking-wet material to retrieve her phone. "This better not be Des, requesting our attendance at a crime scene. I'd prefer to dry off before we step outside again."

"You won't know until you answer it. Make it quick, the anticipation is killing me."

Sam pulled a face at him and glanced down at her phone once it was free. "Strange, it's Rhys. It's not like him to call me out of the blue like this." She wiped the excess rain from her hand and answered the call. "Hey, is everything all right, sweetheart?"

"Sam… Sam… I need you."

The fear in his tone made her heart skip several beats. Tears immediately sprang to her eyes, and she stared at Bob who instantly frowned and mouthed to ask if everything was okay.

She shook her head. "Where are you?"

"I'm outside my building. I can't make it inside. I'm injured. An ambulance is on the way."

"Shit! We can be there in ten minutes. Can you get out of the rain?"

"No."

"Bugger. Stay on the line, don't hang up on me. Bob will drive us."

They ran back to the car. Bob jumped behind the steering wheel, and without a second thought cursed Sam for being shorter than him as he adjusted the driver's seat. He reversed, narrowly missing the car which had just drawn up and was parking a few spaces away. He put his foot down.

"Stay with me, Rhys. Can you tell me what happened?"

"Someone attacked me."

"Why?"

"For being me."

"What do you mean? For being a man, or do you mean for being a psychiatrist?"

"The latter. Damn, I rang for the ambulance a good five minutes before I bothered you. What's taking them so long?"

"Try and remain calm. What injuries do you have, love?"

"The bloke stabbed me after he knocked me to the ground."

"My God! Where?"

"Outside my office, I already told you that," Rhys snapped.

"Keep calm. No, I meant where did he stab you?"

"In the side. I felt the blade scrape against my ribs as he removed the knife."

"Jesus, are you bleeding much?" She closed her eyes, expecting to receive another backlash.

"Enough. My pulse is getting weaker, Sam. Just hurry."

Sam had hit the speaker button. Hearing the news, Bob switched on the blues and twos and slammed his foot down hard on the accelerator. They both shot forward in their seats. Sam offered her partner a reassuring smile and nodded, urging him to get there ASAP. By this time, her stomach had tied itself into a huge knot and her heart was pounding against her ribs.

"We're going as fast as we can. Is there anyone else around who can help you, love?"

"No one. I've tried to pull myself under the tree, but it's not providing the cover I need."

His voice was growing weaker by the second. She gestured for Bob to go faster. He didn't let her down.

"Keep talking to me, Rhys. We're a few minutes away from you."

"I think I can hear a siren in the distance. Is that you or the ambulance?"

"Possibly us. Hang in there." It was all she could think of to say, what with him fading fast. She should have been asking him more questions about his attacker; instead, she concentrated on keeping him conscious and talking.

"Sam, I want you to know…"

"Rhys, stay with us. Don't leave me… Sweetheart, we're almost there now. Rhys. Rhys!"

"Sam, don't you crumble on me," Bob warned. "Stay strong. I'm getting us there as fast as I can. Two streets away and we'll be with him."

Tears pricked her eyes and threatened to fall. She swallowed down the lump that had formed in her throat. "Did you hear that, Rhys? We'll be with you soon."

"Sam…" Rhys whispered.

The lack of clarity in his voice made her reach out and squeeze Bob's hand.

She covered the mouthpiece of the phone. "Hurry, Bob. He needs our help," she whispered. Her mind raced. She pushed away any thoughts of losing him. He meant more to her than any other man she'd known.

Bob screeched around the next corner, flinging them across the road as the tyres failed to grip the tarmac in the torrential rain still lashing down. Sam clung to her seat. Bob muttered an apology and righted the car, setting off again in the correct lane. Luckily, there was little to no traffic on the road, otherwise a second ambulance might have been needed. He carefully rounded the bend at the top of the road and drew up outside Rhys' building where his practice was based.

"Over there!" Bob pointed.

They flung their respective doors open and sprinted to the spot where Rhys was lying, not caring whether they both got wet or not as the rain hadn't let up and was still coming down in biblical fashion.

"Is he alive?" Sam asked after Bob reached Rhys before her.

Bob placed two fingers on Rhys' neck and nodded. "There's a faint pulse. I can hear the ambulance; they're not far now, Sam. Talk to him, reassure him everything is going to be all right."

Sam got down beside him, her knees sinking into the mud on either side of the tree's roots. She pressed her hands over the wound to try and prevent him losing any more blood. "Rhys, I'm here, baby. You're doing great. The paramedics are nearly here. Another few minutes and they'll be with us."

Bob jumped to his feet the second the ambulance drew to a halt. He ran to apprise the emergency staff of what was going on and then bounded back to join Sam. "They'll be here soon; they're collecting their equipment from the back." He tugged on Sam's arm as the older male paramedic approached them.

"Stand clear, we've got this."

Bob yanked on her arm a second time. The rest of what happened over the next couple of minutes was played out in slow motion for Sam.

"Please, we're both police officers. This is DI Cobbs' other half. He's been stabbed. We've been speaking to him over the phone for the past ten minutes. He's been getting weaker and weaker in that time. You have to help him," Bob pleaded with the female paramedic as she appeared, carrying two bags of equipment.

"We'll do our very best for him. Stand back, we need room to work. What's his name?"

"It's Rhys Wilkins," Sam replied.

Bob hooked an arm around Sam's shoulders and pulled her close to him. He kissed her on the temple and tried his best to comfort her. "He's in safe hands now, Sam. They've got this."

"I can't lose him, Bob. I just can't." She stared down at the man she'd barely known two years, who had stolen her heart the minute his piercing blue eyes had looked at her.

Bob placed a finger under her chin and forced her attention on him. "Stop it. You're not going to lose him. You hear me?"

"I hope not. Shit, what about Casper? Where's the dog? He always walks Casper at lunchtime."

"We'll worry about that later. He won't have gone far."

Sam wriggled out of Bob's grasp and spun around three hundred and sixty degrees. "He's nowhere to be seen."

"You're not thinking straight, Sam. Calm down, let's deal with Rhys first. Once he's on his way to hospital, we'll search for Casper."

Sam removed her phone from her soaking-wet jacket, praying the water hadn't seeped through any of the joints, and dialled Rhys' office number. It took a few rings, but eventually his secretary picked up. "Brenda, it's Sam. Is Casper there with you?"

"Sorry, who?"

"Sam, Rhys' other half. It's important, is Casper in the office?"

"Yes, sorry, you caught me on the hop there. Casper is lying in his basket, but Rhys is out."

"I know. There's been an incident. We're outside the building now. Will you keep Casper safe until I can swing by and pick him up later?"

"Of course. Is everything all right, Sam?"

"No. Not wishing to alarm you, but Rhys has been stabbed. I'm going to the hospital with him. You're going to need to cancel his appointments for the rest of the day. Can you do that for me?"

"Oh my. Is Rhys okay?"

"He's weak. The paramedics are with him at present. Is there any way you can take Casper home with you?"

"Absolutely. You deal with Rhys. I've got your number; I'll give you a call later. Send him my love, won't you?"

"I will. You're a star, thanks, Brenda. I'll be in touch soon."

"I'll be thinking of you both. This is just dreadful."

"I'll need to speak with you later, once I know Rhys is okay."

"No problem. I'll make the calls and head home. Don't worry about Casper, he'll be safe with me. Monty, my Staffy, will take him under his wing when we get home. They get on great together."

"That's brilliant, thanks, hon." Sam ended her call. She shuddered as the rain dripped down her neck and soaked through to her undergarments. "It's going to take us hours to dry off."

"That's the least of our worries," Bob said. He took a step forward. "How is he doing? Is he going to make it?"

The male paramedic stared up at him and winced. "We're doing our best, but I have to warn you, at this stage, it's touch and go."

Sam trembled uncontrollably. It felt like the hand of Satan had entered her chest and ripped her heart out.

CHAPTER 1

Bob had taken over the reins at the station for her while she'd kept vigil at Rhys' bedside. The staff had insisted that she should go home and get some rest, however, knowing that Vernon, her brother-in-law, was looking after Sonny and Casper, their two dogs, was a load off her mind. She couldn't face going home to the empty house when Rhys was here, still fighting for his life. Nothing else mattered to her, not right now. He was her everything. Without him being a constant in her life, she no longer had an existence.

The consultant requested to see her at the nurses' station. Reluctantly, she left Rhys' bedside, but not before she leaned over and kissed him on the cheek. Leaving the private room he was in, she thrust her shoulders back and walked towards the young male consultant, who was already checking his watch whilst awaiting her arrival.

"Ah, there you are, Miss Cobbs."

She didn't correct him, tell him her real title. What was the point? She doubted if it would hold much clout around here, on his turf. She could see in his eyes what he thought of her; he regarded her as a sniffling relative who was probably going to have another meltdown as soon as he opened his mouth. She was eager to prove him wrong and swallowed down the acid burning her throat. "What news do you have for me, Doctor?"

"It's as we expected. He has a ruptured liver and some worrying internal bleeding. We're unsure how that has occurred. I've been in touch with one of the best surgeons in the area. He's presently on duty at Newcastle Hospital until nine-thirty this evening, then he's going to jump in a helicopter and be with us by eleven at the latest. Rhys will be operated on as soon as Mr Myers gets here."

"Not wishing to speak out of turn, but won't Mr Myers be too tired to operate by then?"

Doctor Sidwell cocked an eyebrow. "You let us worry about that. We're treating Rhys' injuries as serious, that's all you need to know."

"Thanks, that told me," she mumbled.

"I'm sorry. I have other patients to see, forgive me for running out on you like this. I thought it was important to bring you up to date on where things stand. All I can do is assure you that Rhys is in the best hands possible. At present he's stable, and I stand by my decision to ask Mr Myers to assist us in the operation. I'll be in touch with you tomorrow. My suggestion would be that you go home and get some rest, if it's your intention to be here later this evening, during your partner's operation."

"I'll hang around, if you don't mind. Just in case Rhys regains consciousness."

"If that's your decision and you're going against my advice, there's nothing further for me to say. I'll bid you good day and get on with my rounds."

Sam watched him walk away. She couldn't help feeling five inches tall as her eyes bored into his departing back. *I'm too tired to be bothered with this. All I care about is whether Rhys recovers or not. It's not worth falling out with the hospital staff, if I want to remain by his bedside.*

Her mobile rang. Bob's number showed up on the screen. "Hey, just checking in to see how you're doing."

Mental and physical exhaustion suddenly overwhelmed her. She fell into the chair beside her. "Hi, I'm doing okay. How are you?"

"Stop kidding a kidder, Sam. Tell me the truth."

"I wish I knew what that was. I've just this minute spoken with the consultant who told me their intention is to operate on Rhys this evening. Apparently, one of the best surgeons in the business is coming over from Newcastle by chopper to do the deed."

"Shit, what are you saying? That he's still in danger?"

"According to the consultant, yes. I'm so exhausted I can't think straight, Bob. All I know is that Rhys is still out cold. I've been sitting with him all this time, and he hasn't stirred once in the last twenty-four hours."

"Isn't that intentional? Didn't they up his medication to ensure he didn't regain consciousness so that his body would have time to heal properly?"

"Don't ask me, my mind is a blur, partner. If that's what I've already told you then it must be the truth."

"Sam, you're worrying me. You need to go home and get some rest. You're not doing either of you any favours. Rhys is going to be reliant on you when he wakes up."

Tears emerged and stung her eyes. "If he wakes up," she whispered, the words catching in her throat.

"I'm coming over there. Sod work, you need me by your side. I won't be long."

Sam didn't have the energy to argue with him. She ended the call and placed her head in her hands. One of the nurses, about to go off duty, found her still sobbing five minutes later, and she sat down beside Sam.

"Oh, Sam. What's all this? He's doing better than any of us could have anticipated. You must hold on to that."

Tears staining her cheeks, Sam glanced up and swallowed. "Do I? Is he? What else am I to think? He's been unconscious for a while, and now the consultant is telling me his life is still in the balance and he's due to have an emergency operation this evening."

"He is? That's great news. They wouldn't be operating if they didn't feel his body could take it, Sam."

"Really? I'm all over the place. I just need him to wake up, tell me he's all right."

"That will come, eventually. My advice would be to go home and get some proper rest for a few hours. I can give you a lift, if you want?"

"That's very kind of you, but no, I want to stay here, with him. I'll try and get some sleep in the room."

The kind nurse patted her on the knee and stood. "Don't forget we're here for you as much as for Rhys. We appreciate how difficult this is for the families concerned. Don't be afraid to reach out to us if you need anything, you hear me?"

"Thank you. I will. Enjoy your time off."

The nurse smiled. "I doubt it. I'm off to pick up my two-year-old from my mother's now. What's that saying again? Ah, yes, no rest for the wicked."

Sam smiled and shook her head. "Not sure how you cope working here full-time and having a toddler at home."

"Needs must. My husband walked out on me the minute I found out I was pregnant."

"What? Why? Sorry, that's the detective in me being nosey."

"Children weren't part of our future, at least that's what he told me."

"And did you agree to that when you married him?"

"Did I heck? I don't recall the subject ever coming up. Hey, I didn't mean to burden you with my sob story. Believe me, I'm better off without him. My daughter and I have a blast, most of the time, and Mum and Dad always chip in, too. If I didn't have them around, it would be a different story entirely."

"Hang on to them for as long as you can. I sadly lost my mother a little while ago."

"You have had a rough time of it, haven't you? Sorry, love. Get some rest, I'll see you tomorrow."

"Thanks, have a good day yourself, or try to."

"Don't worry about me, I have my day already mapped out ahead of time, most days." She waved and headed down the corridor towards the lift.

Sam sat there, considering what the nurse had told her about her own dire straits, and it turned out to be the kick up the arse she needed to get her act together. She'd been too maudlin since she'd arrived. Wallowing hopelessly in her own self-pity, when she should be out there, with her partner, hunting down the person who had attacked Rhys and put his life in danger.

I need to think positively about the outcome of the operation. Rhys didn't die, he might not be in the best of health right now, but at least he's still with me. His fighting spirit will ensure he sticks around for a while yet.

She had contacted his parents, but they were both too busy with their work to make the trek down from Scotland to visit him. Sam couldn't believe it when his mother, a renowned heart consultant in Edinburgh, had told her to keep them informed. She knew they were in constant contact with the medical staff; maybe she should take something from that.

If Rhys was that bad, they'd both be here sitting beside him, wouldn't they?

Sam sat in the corridor for another ten minutes, until Bob came hurtling out of the lift towards her. He took one look at her tear-stained cheeks, and she could tell he was thinking the worst.

"Oh God. I'm not too late, am I?"

She hugged him and whispered in his ear, "No, he's still with us. This is me being silly, having a meltdown."

He gripped the tops of her arms and pushed her away from him. "Hey, you're entitled to have one, if Rhys is still bad. Haven't his blasted parents shown up yet?"

"No. They're being kept up to date with his progress. I spoke to his father yesterday; he assured me they were doing all they could to clear their busy schedules and would be here soon."

"Christ, if you can't 'clear your busy schedule' when your son's life is hanging in the balance, when can you? That's just not right, you shouldering all of this by yourself, Sam."

She offered up a weak smile. "Don't worry about me, I'll be fine. Any news for me?"

"Yes, as it happens, there is. We've been trawling through the CCTV footage of the area around Rhys' building, and we've managed to find the attack. It's not pleasant."

"Tell me... I need to know how this occurred, Bob, and don't hold back. Do that and I'll never forgive you."

"Okay, but I'm going to need you to remain calm. The last thing I want to do is upset you any more than you are already."

She folded her arms and tapped her foot. "Will you get on with it?"

"You're still as impatient as ever. I'm doing my best not to burden you here, and you're having none of it, are you?"

"You and I are going to fall out if you don't tell me."

Bob took a step back and raised his hands. "You're never going to change, even though you've got a mountain of worry on your plate at the moment."

"Sounds about right. Hit me with it."

"Okay, but I'm stating now that I'm telling you this against my better judgement."

"Whatever."

Sam sat, and Bob did the same but left an empty chair between them.

"We've got the footage of Rhys returning to the building. He'd been to the baker's to collect his lunch; we found that out from Brenda, his secretary."

"I know who she is, stop talking to me as though I'm an idiot instead of your boss. Get to the facts, Bob, before I scream the hospital down."

"Gee, you can be so infuriating at times."

"You took the words right out of my mouth," she shot back swiftly. "So, he was carrying his lunch back to his office… and?"

"And, out of nowhere, someone dressed all in black, with their hood up, ran at him, a knife in their right hand raised above their head. Rhys dropped the bag and held his hands up, obviously trying to talk the person down."

"What about witnesses? Was there anyone else around at that time?"

"No, that's the thing I found weird. It's usually quite a busy area, offices all around, and the footfall in that part is normally pretty hectic, but nothing."

Sam placed her thumb and finger around her chin. "That is strange. Might be worth further investigation."

"Don't worry, I've got Liam and Oliver out there now, checking all the offices in the surrounding area in the hope that someone might have been looking out of the window at the time the incident took place."

"What else did the cameras pick up?"

"Rhys trying to talk to the person, possibly pleading for his life."

"God, he must have been terrified. My heart goes out to him. He's a man of words, not equipped to deal with dangerous situations, unlike us."

"He appeared to be doing okay, for a few minutes. His attacker kept a watchful eye out for what was going on behind him. It was during one of those times that Rhys took a few steps towards him. He made the wrong move; his actions appeared to anger his attacker, who ran at him and knifed him a couple of times."

"Hmm… they only said he had one injury, that was to his liver, but they've since told me he has internal bleeding. You'd think they would know how many knife wounds he had, wouldn't you?"

Bob shrugged. "Very strange. Maybe the first one only nicked him in the side. It was too far away to tell, really. Anyway, Rhys dropped to his knees, and the perp towered over him, shouting in his face for a few seconds before he ran off."

Sam shook her head as she contemplated the scene. "And all this went on without a single witness being present? That's what I'm struggling to get my head around here. I wonder if Rhys knew him. If his attacker was one of his patients or clients, or whatever you want to call him."

"I've got Suzanna on that. Sent her off to question Brenda, who is an utter mess."

"That's understandable. I sent Vernon to collect Casper. She took him home with her for a few hours after the incident happened, and he said she was in tears and not making any sense the whole time he was there."

"It must have been a real shock for her, if he only popped to the shop to pick up some lunch."

"Why would this person choose to hurt Rhys? He's such a likeable, inoffensive kind of chap, and yet, here he is, twenty-four hours or so later, fighting for his life in a hospital bed. None of this is making any sense."

"I know it doesn't. As a team, we're doing our best to find the reason behind the attack."

"What's the chief had to say about this?"

"He's told us to do what's necessary to find the culprit over the next couple of days."

"And what then? What if it takes longer to find the bastard?"

Bob hitched up a shoulder. "Your guess is as good as mine. That's why we're all giving it one hundred percent for you, Sam. We want this dickhead caught as much as you do."

"I doubt it," she replied. She clenched and unclenched her fists. "I should be out there, not sitting around here…"

"Hey, you trained us well. Let the team do the necessary with regard to the case, you do what you have to do about Rhys getting better."

"That's the frustrating part, all I'm doing is sitting here, staring at the walls most of the time. If I leave him, that's going to look bad on me with the nursing staff. I'm in a no-win situation, and I detest it."

"Trust us. If the information is out there, we'll find it."

Sam reached out a hand to him. "You've never let me down in the past."

He took it and squeezed it tightly.

She sighed. "There was definitely only one attacker? No one waiting in the wings? Did you follow him on the cameras? See which way he set off in?"

"Are you expecting me to answer all those questions at the same time?"

She smiled. "Sorry. Just eager to get on top of the case, you know me."

"I should do by now. Right, here goes. In answer to your first question, there appears to be only one attacker. We didn't spot anyone else lingering at the time of the attack, but they might have been out of shot, who knows? We traced his movements through a few streets, and then he just disappeared."

"If he had an accomplice, they might have picked him up, out of view of the camera."

"I've got that angle covered. Alex is back at the station, still going over the footage with Claire."

"Good, Claire will keep him on track, she won't take any of his bullshit, and no, don't tell him I said that."

Bob smiled. "As if I would. I think I've answered all your questions now, haven't I? We've got this, Sam. The last thing we need is for you to start worrying if we're doing our jobs right. Oh, and the chief asked me to pass on his regards. He told me to tell you to ring him when you know something definite about Rhys' condition."

"I won't know anything until after the operation. I'll give him a call tomorrow, not sure if he'll appreciate me waking him up in the early hours of the morning."

Bob sniggered. "Yeah, you might want to hold off doing that to him, that is, if you value your job."

She squeezed his hand. "Thanks for coming, Bob. You've successfully cheered me up. I was in a very dark place before you arrived."

"I know. We're partners for a reason. You've always been more than a boss to me, Sam."

She rose from her seat and pulled him to his feet then hugged him. "Thank you, I feel the same way about you. Now get out of here. I'll be in touch in the morning, once I know how the operation went."

"I'll hold you to that. We're all behind you. Don't ever think you have to handle this burden alone, even if his parents can't be arsed coming down here to lend their support."

She pulled away from him. "They're professional people, I accept that."

He cocked an eyebrow. "What? And you're not? You're still here, and this is over twenty-four hours after he was admitted."

She grinned. "People react in different ways when something like this lands on their doorstep. You know what I say, my conscience is always clear. I suggest you ask them if they feel the same way."

"I'd rather steer clear of them if it's all the same to you. Do you think they would have shown up if he'd died?"

Sam closed her eyes and shook her head. "That's something I'd rather not think about."

"Maybe you should. We all need to know if our parents have our backs at a time like this."

"They love him, in their own way, hon. Still, that's my concern, not yours. You have enough on your plate to contend with. It's fortunate we're not in the middle of another investigation right now."

"Yep, we need to count our blessings with that one. It's good that we can devote the time to finding this prick. I can't promise I'll be able to show restraint once we pull him in for questioning."

"You'll be fine. I'm hoping to be back at work within a day or two. I can help restraining you."

Bob kissed her on the cheek. "There's an answer to that one, but I think I'll leave it dangling all the same."

"Get out of here. Good luck, I'll be in touch when I can."

"You can text me. I often wake up during the night for a pee anyway. Or is that too much information?"

"Somewhat. Take care and thank the team for all the effort they're putting in to finding this scumbag."

He set off up the corridor and shouted over his shoulder, "That goes without saying. Get some rest, you look… terrible."

"Funny how you never mentioned that when you were standing a few feet away from me."

"I'm not stupid."

Sam laughed; it felt good after suffering from the gloomy disposition she'd been in since Rhys was admitted to hospital. She waved at him as the lift doors closed and he blew her a kiss. She went back in the private room to fetch her handbag. She paused to stand beside Rhys, sending out a silent plea, not for the first time, for him to pull through, then she strolled down the corridor to the canteen.

The young woman behind the counter smiled and asked, "What can I get you?"

"I can't remember the last time I ate. What do you recommend?"

"The mac and cheese is always a winner."

"Mac and cheese it is then, plus a flat white, thank you."

"Pay at the end and take a seat, I'll bring it over to you."

Sam paid for her food and chose a table close to the window. She glanced around. Some of the other diners checked their phones and others stared at their half-eaten plates of food, making her wonder if those people were in a similar situation to hers. The rain battered the window beside her, drawing her attention back to the dreary day outside. That would have matched her mood an hour ago, before Bob had raised her spirits when he'd visited her.

"Here you go, I gave you an extra spoonful. Don't let on or I'll get into trouble."

Sam smiled up at her. "You're too kind. I hope I can manage it."

"You look as though you're in need of feeding up… oops, that was a personal comment, I'm sorry."

"You didn't offend me. It's been an horrendous time, and I admit this is the first decent meal I've eaten in that time." She stuck her fork in and sampled the pasta dish. "You were right to recommend it, it's delicious."

"Glad you like it. I make it myself with love and care every morning."

"Wow, are you the chef?"

"Not really. I'm a kitchen hand but I made the chef my mac and cheese once, when someone was off sick. He thought it was incredible, so he asked me to keep it on the daily menu. You looked sad when you came in, I hope your day improves."

"I'm sure it will once I've eaten my meal. Thank you for taking the time out of your day to check on me, it's appreciated." Sam sighed and felt the need to fill the young woman in about why she was there. "My fella was stabbed by a stranger yesterday. He's unconscious and is due to have an emergency operation later."

The young woman placed a gentle hand on Sam's shoulder. "Oh dear, I'm so sorry. Thank you for sharing that with me. I went through something similar with my brother a few years ago. A random attack in the nightclub. Someone stabbed him in the back. It was over a girl they both were keen to make a move on, apparently."

"Ouch, I hope your brother survived?"

The woman's chin dipped. "He did, but now he's paralysed and is confined to a wheelchair."

"Goodness me, how dreadful. I'm so sorry to hear that."

"He's a better person than me. His spirit is always buoyant, and he tells me off when I get down days. It puts life back into perspective when someone has to deal with serious injuries. At the end of the day, these are his words, not mine, he's happy to be here still."

"I suppose it's all about your attitude to life, isn't it?"

"That's right. Try not to let the situation get you down. Wishing your fella well with his operation. I'm sure our paths will cross again in the next few days. I'm Colette by the way."

"Hi, Colette, I'm Sam. Thank you for your reassuring words."

"My pleasure. Enjoy your meal." She smiled and turned on her heel.

Sam's heart felt much lighter after her chat with Colette, and even though she wasn't that hungry when she'd shown up at the canteen, she tucked in and cleared her plate before she'd realised she'd even started her meal. Sam looked over at the counter and caught Colette watching her. Sam held up her plate to show it was empty, and Colette gave her a thumbs-up.

Sam took her time drinking her coffee, not in a rush to get back. Colette startled her a few minutes later when she collected her plate.

"Hungrier than you thought, eh?"

"Hard to leave anything as delicious as that. Compliments to the chef."

Colette's cheeks reddened, and she mumbled a thank you.

"I mean it, you should package it and sell it."

"No chance of that happening. Glad you enjoyed it. I wanted to wish you luck for your fella later. I'm about to go off-duty now."

"Thanks for caring. All the staff have been brilliant at the hospital."

Colette smiled and walked away. Sam finished her coffee and then slowly made her way back to Rhys' room. She spent the next half an hour or so sending texts to members of her family and to Rhys' parents, not that they responded until much later in the day. By that time, Sam had managed to catch a few hours' sleep in the chair. She woke up with a stiff neck and back and checked her phone to find a message from Rhys' mother, which stated she would give Sam a call the next day and that she and her husband would be thinking of their son during his operation.

The matter of fact, possibly tactless text, made Sam angry. She had to step out of the room and pace the corridor for several minutes until she calmed down. Another nurse checked on her a little while later.

"Anxious about the operation, are you?"

"Not really," Sam replied. "More the lack of compassion shown by his parents, if you must know."

"Sorry to hear that. His mother does call us regularly. I get the impression she's a very busy person."

"Aren't we all? Sorry, I didn't mean to sound off, it's the frustration talking."

"Understandable. He knows you're with him, that's all that will matter to him when he wakes up and finds you sitting alongside him."

"I love him, where else would I be?"

"Exactly. Be kind to yourself. We're all here if you need to vent any time."

"Thank you. I'm hoping things will change once he comes back from the theatre."

"We've all got our fingers crossed for him." The nurse left the room.

Sam moved chairs so she could sit next to Rhys and touched his face. "Please come back to me the way you were, Rhys. The boys and I can't do this alone, we won't be able to live without you." She stared at him, praying to see some kind of reaction from him to let her know that he'd heard and possibly understood her. There was nothing.

. . .

THE HOSPITAL PORTER came to collect him a couple of hours later. He allowed Sam to kiss Rhys and wish him luck before he wheeled his bed out of the room. Sitting there, alone, she felt bereft. She hated the quietness surrounding her and the way her thoughts kept running away from her, so she decided to walk the length and breadth of the hospital to pass the time. The nurse on duty promised to text her the moment Rhys was back in his room.

Walking eased the pain in her joints. She wasn't used to sitting around for hours on end. However, it didn't rid her of the intense, dark thoughts filling her tired mind. Thoughts of Rhys dying in the operating theatre. Tears were her constant companion throughout her journey. She battled relentlessly to keep them under control but mostly failed.

The text she'd been expecting came through when she was at the far end of the hospital. It read, *Rhys is out of surgery and in the recovery room. They'll monitor him there for a few hours and then return him to the ward.*

That's it? Nothing about how successful the surgery has been? What am I to think about that? Should I be worried, are they keeping something from me?

The questions kept coming, until her head appeared to swell to double its normal size. She took a moment to sit and consider what would happen next, if Rhys didn't regain consciousness.

No, I can't. I refuse to consider that. He's going to make it, he has to. We need him.

She bought a coffee from a nearby vending machine and stared into it for the next twenty minutes, trying to answer some of the questions running through her mind.

Enough is enough, I need to get out of here and back to the ward, where I belong. Correction, I need to get Rhys back home where he belongs, with the boys fussing over him. That's what will make him better. Who am I kidding? Only the doctors have the ability to make him better, not us.

She threw her empty cup in the bin and began the slow walk back through the long, winding corridors, stopping now and again to read an information sign that could one day save someone's life. Although Sam read the one about giving some CPR in an emergency, the specifics refused to sink in.

When she reached the room, there was a nurse in there but no sign of the love of her life. "Oh, I thought he might have been back by now. Do you know how the operation went?"

"Unfortunately, they never tell us. The consultant will be around to see you first thing in the morning, to share the news."

Sam sat in the chair and buried her head in her hands. She'd never felt so distraught in all her life. Being kept in the dark like this was frustrating the hell out of her. The nurse crossed the room to offer her some comfort.

"Hey, we'll have none of this. Up until now you've shown us nothing but strength, don't let yourself down now. He's had the operation, that can only be seen as a good thing. If he wasn't strong enough, they wouldn't have gone ahead with it. You've got to take heart from that, Sam."

She glanced sideways at the nurse who offered her a tissue. "Thank you. I know what you're saying is right, but I feel utterly helpless—no, it's much worse than that, inadequate, yes, that's the term I'm searching for."

"I can understand that, given the career you've chosen. Sometimes life throws us a curveball now and again. I like to think it's a way of testing us, to see how we react. So far, I'd say you've coped pretty well for someone who hasn't slept in her own bed for a while. I'll tell you this, I wouldn't have had the resilience you've had if my other half was lying unconscious in a hospital bed."

Sam shook her head and smiled. "I doubt if that's true. Nurses are born carers."

"I have to put you right there because, believe me, all our training goes out of the window when a member of our own family has a spell in hospital."

"How long before he comes back, do you know?"

"He's due soon. Why don't I leave you in peace, let you get forty winks before he returns?"

"Thanks, I'll try. I just want to say I appreciate how kind and thoughtful you and your colleagues have been."

The nurse smiled and patted her on the arm. "We're only doing our job. Get some rest, while you still can."

A FEW HOURS LATER, the sound of the door opening startled Sam out of her sleep. She must have drifted off, despite her extreme efforts to remain awake. She shot out of her chair to assist the porter to put the bed back into its correct position.

"Here he is, back safe and sound," the porter said cheerfully.

"Has he woken up at all?"

The porter shook his head. "Sorry, I think it's still too early for that. I must go now. He's going to be fine, I can sense it here." He held a hand over his heart.

"I hope you're right. Thank you."

The tall black man left the room, and as the silence descended again, Sam felt lost and alone once more. She tried to kick the feeling of doom surrounding her, but it proved pointless. She stood and studied Rhys. Touched the extra wrinkles by his eyes that she didn't remember being there before his operation, or was she just imagining that?

Her phone pinged to announce that a message had

arrived. Sam opened it to find that Rhys' mother was asking how the surgery had gone. She took a photo of Rhys, hoping that would change his parents' minds about travelling to visit their son, and sent it along with a message, that the consultant would tell her in the morning how the operation went.

His mother didn't respond.

Sam refused to allow herself to get angry. Instead, she sat beside Rhys, his hand in both of hers, and prayed for him to pull through his ordeal.

It turned out to be one of the longest nights ever for Sam. The not knowing had played on her mind constantly, hampering her ability to catch up on her sleep. The following morning, Doctor Sidwell stopped by for the briefest of visits to share the news she'd been desperate to hear.

"The operation was a success. The surgeon managed to stop the bleeding; there was another tear that the MRI scan failed to detect."

"When can I expect him to wake up?"

The doctor shrugged. "Your guess is as good as mine. I'll drop by and see him later. You look exhausted, you should have followed my advice and gone home last night."

"I wanted to stay with him," Sam snapped. "I'm sorry, you didn't deserve that."

"Exhaustion makes us say and do things that we wouldn't necessarily consider doing ordinarily. I don't know how many more times I have to tell you this, Rhys is in safe hands. I repeat, you should go home and get some proper rest, you'll be no good to him when he wakes up if you don't."

"Thanks for your advice, but I've come this far without leaving his side."

"That's your prerogative," he said and left the room.

Sam pulled a face at the door as it closed behind him and

flopped into the chair beside Rhys. "Come back to me, love. Open your eyes. Show me you're still able to hear me, sense that I'm around you."

Her gaze ran the length of his body and caught a movement in his finger. She clutched his hand between hers and spoke gently to him. "Rhys, sweetheart, can you hear me?"

His finger twitched again. She ran out of the room to inform the nurse on duty who returned with her.

"Let's check his vital signs."

His finger twitched a third time.

"Did you see that?" Sam shouted excitedly. She covered her mouth with her hand. "Sorry, I mean, it wasn't my imagination, was it? There was movement there, wasn't there?"

"I can confirm it wasn't your imagination. I believe he's coming around, Sam. Keep talking to him."

"Rhys, I'm here for you. Casper and Sonny send lots of kisses your way, they're desperate to see you."

The nurse smiled, made some notes on the chart at the bottom of his bed and left her to it.

Sam towered over him, kissed his cheeks and ran a hand around his face. His eyes flickered and opened. "Oh my God. Rhys, you're back. How are you feeling?"

He ran his tongue around his lips. She poured some water from the jug on the bedside table and offered him a drink. His lips appeared to be stuck together, so she ran a wet finger around them then offered the glass up to his mouth again. This time he took a sip but coughed and spluttered a little. Sam rang the buzzer, and the nurse entered the room.

"Ah, you're awake. How are you feeling, Rhys?" the nurse asked. She peered at her watch and took his pulse.

"Like I got hit by a train. Can I go home now?"

"Not yet. You've had a major operation. Once you've recovered from that, I get the sense there will be no stopping you. Give me a shout if you need me."

Sam didn't say a word, she couldn't, she was in shock, knowing that he had survived.

"Hey, why are you crying?" he asked and touched a hand clumsily to her cheek, bashing her nose in the process. "Sorry, my coordination is in the toilet."

"It's the relief of having you back with us. Don't worry about me."

"I do. You're all I ever worry about, DI Sam Cobbs."

"Bless you, you need to stop doing that. Can you remember what happened?" she asked, eager to hear what he knew, if anything, about his assailant.

He tipped his head back against his pillow and closed his eyes. "Of course I can."

"Are you strong enough to tell me? The team have been doing their best to find the perpetrator, but without knowing all the facts, it's proving difficult."

"I don't know him. He was quite young, I suppose in his late teens."

"Why did he attack you? Do you know?"

"I'm tired, Sam."

"Okay, we can leave it for now. Get some sleep."

He didn't hear her, he'd already drifted off again. She placed her head on his chest to make sure he was still breathing, delighted to listen to his heart beating. A few moments later, she returned to her seat and fell asleep.

RHYS WOKE her up about an hour later, crying out in his sleep. He had tears running down his cheeks. Sam tried to comfort him, but he pushed her arms away. She feared he was probably reliving the attack and thought she must have been the perpetrator. She could tell it was going to be a long road for him, for both of them.

The doctor entered the room not long after. "Ah, I was

told he had regained consciousness." He moved towards the bed. "Has he been crying?"

"Yes, I think he had a nightmare, probably reliving the attack."

"That's common. Did he speak to you much when he woke up?"

"Not really. He grew tired quickly. When will he be able to come home?"

"That seems a pretty naïve question at this stage. Let's not push things. He'll need time to recover more before we can consider discharging him." He gave her a curt nod and walked out of the room.

Rude man! Sam spent the next few minutes sending a copy-and-pasted text to her family and his, telling them that he had woken up but had now drifted off to sleep again. She was hit by 'great news' messages from everyone except his parents, which narked the hell out of her all over again.

What the fuck is wrong with them? I haven't been home since the incident, and in that time, I've received the minimal amount of contact from them. What's the point in me messaging them? I can see now why Rhys chose to settle in Cumbria and doesn't speak about them often, let alone visit them.

She stepped outside the room and rang Bob. "Hi, I was just checking in with you, see how things are going?"

"We're getting there. Thanks for the text earlier. I let the team know he was on the mend."

"A slight improvement is better than none at all. Any news for me?"

"Not really. We're piecing things together. I don't suppose Rhys has given you any clues as to who the culprit was yet, has he?"

"I managed to get out of him that his attacker was young."

"I kind of figured as much, going by what he was wearing."

"He fell asleep not long after, exhausted, and then had a nightmare. I think he was probably reliving the attack."

"Shit. It's going to take a while for him to get over it. Is there anything we can do to help, Sam?"

"Apart from tracking down and arresting the perpetrator, no, nothing, hon."

"You sound tired. Have you managed to get any sleep yet?"

"I've caught forty winks here and there. Now that he's out of danger, I think I'm going to go home tonight, get some proper sleep, in my own bed. Of course, that depends on how he gets on during the day. If he starts going backwards then I'll stay with him."

"Sounds like you need a good sleep. He'll be fine where he is, Sam. You said yourself that he appears to be out of danger now."

"Is that you nagging me, partner?"

"Not at all. You know I'm talking a lot of sense. Let the staff take care of him while you look after yourself. Go home and have a nice long soak in the bath, that usually puts the world back on track for my missus."

"I'll see how the day goes. I might even consider coming back to work tomorrow. I've missed you guys."

"Are you nuts? You don't want to do that yet. I've got things covered here, I promise. I'm even on top of all your mail, too."

"Wonders will never cease. Maybe I'll take a month off, see how you cope then."

"Christ, don't even jest about that. A week is my limit. I've made it a priority this time around, only to ease it for you on your return. I'm not saying I've dealt with everything, just some of it."

"Ah, and here we have it, the truth at last." Sam laughed. "Honestly, it's fine, whatever you've managed to do will be a huge help to me. What I need you and the team to do is concentrate all your efforts on finding the bastard who did this to Rhys. At this point, we still don't know if he's going to make a full recovery or not."

"Jesus, that's tough, Sam. I'm sure he's going to pull through and be back to his normal cheerful self soon."

"I've got everything crossed. I'll give you a call later, let you know if I've decided to stay here another night or not."

"You'll never listen to the advice handed out to you, will you?"

"Goodbye, partner." She ended the call and rested her head back against the wall and closed her eyes.

One of the nurses found her in the same position a few minutes later. She tapped her on the shoulder and asked, "Are you all right, Sam?"

"Sorry, yes. I've been in touch with friends and family, now I'm trying to decide whether I should go home tonight or not."

"I would. It makes sense. And I'm sure your dogs will be missing you."

"But what if Rhys thinks I've deserted him?"

"He won't. I promise you. In my experience, he'll be drifting in and out of sleep for days yet. You can trust us to take care of him."

"I know that, I just don't want him feeling that I've deserted him. I suppose my indecision stems from his parents not being here."

The nurse shrugged. "It's hard making that decision when you live so far away. Don't fall out with them about this, Sam, it's not what Rhys would want."

"I agree. It doesn't prevent me from getting annoyed about it, though. After all, I've only known him a couple of years, they've known him all his life."

"Nowt so queer as folk, as the saying goes. Give me a shout if you need anything."

"I will. Thanks." Sam stepped back into the room to find Rhys still gently snoring. She rang her brother-in-law to check on the dogs. "Hi, Vernon, how's it going?"

"These two are a breeze to look after, Sam. How are things at the hospital?"

"So-so. I think I'm going to chance leaving here tonight and go home."

"That's cool. Do you want me to drop the dogs off for you?"

"Would you mind? I've missed them so much. I just wish I could bring them in to visit Rhys. His recovery would improve if he had them by his side."

"I hate to tell you this, but that's never going to happen, sweetheart. Why don't you give me a call later, in case you have a change of heart? I've got nothing planned, except a walk up the lake this afternoon. I thought I'd pop in to The Gather while I'm up there."

"Now I'm envious. Will you say hi to Emma and the staff up there for me? Tell them we'll pay them a visit soon, once Rhys is on the mend."

"I'll do that. Take care, love. I'm always here if you need me."

"I know and I appreciate it more than you realise, Vernon. Everyone has been so supportive. Speak later."

"What do you expect? We think the world of you guys."

Sam blew him a kiss and hung up.

LATER THAT EVENING, with Rhys only waking up once during the afternoon, she made the final decision to return home. She rang Vernon to let him know that she was leaving, and he and

Crystal met her at the house with a welcome takeaway. She filled up when the dogs ran towards her. Sonny jumped up, knocking her sideways, and she ended up on her backside. She buried her face in his fur, and the tears came. Casper, despite still being a pup, was the more chilled of the two dogs. He licked her face then ran back to Vernon who threw the ball for him to chase.

Sam kissed the top of her dog's head. "I bet Doreen has missed you, Sonny."

Her neighbour looked after Sonny every day, while Sam was at work. Doreen had waved at Sam from her lounge window when she had arrived home, but Sam didn't get the chance to bring her neighbour up to date on Rhys' condition because Vernon and Crystal had drawn up right behind her. Sam made a note to drop in and see Doreen later, after her sister and brother-in-law departed for the evening, if she wasn't too tired.

"I might be speaking out of turn here," Crystal said as they tucked in to their sweet-and-sour chicken with noodles.

"Leave it, Crystal," Vernon warned.

"I can't. She needs to know what I think about Rhys' parents."

Sam smiled. "Honestly, love, you can't tell me anything I haven't thought myself since he was admitted."

Crystal squeezed Sam's hand. "It's appalling, them keeping their distance at a time like this. What if he hadn't made it?"

Sam shrugged. "I reckon they would have blamed me if he'd died."

"No way. Why? None of this is your fault, is it?"

"I don't think so. As far as I know, the attack happened because of who he is, or more to the point, what his occupation is."

"Really? Do you think it was one of his patients?" Vernon asked.

Sam sipped at her wine. "There's every possibility of that. My team have done their best to identify the culprit, but his disguise on the footage has left them scratching their heads."

"So, what's the answer?" Crystal asked through a mouthful of noodles.

"I guess I'll find out tomorrow."

"What? You can't be serious? You're truly thinking about returning to work tomorrow?"

Sam nodded and pushed her plate away. "I have to, with one sole purpose in mind…"

"To find the perp," Vernon finished for her.

"You've got it. I think Doreen will be okay with the dogs, I'll have a word with her later."

"Sorry, I have a meeting with the boss at midday. I can always come by afterwards and take them both out for a long walk to tire them out."

"Would you? That would be fantastic, Vernon. You're the best."

"Hey, it's what we do for those we care about. You've got this, Sam. Rhys will be back home with you soon enough."

"I hope so. I really do, because I don't mind telling you that I'm lost without him."

Crystal left her seat and pulled Sam to her feet. "Now stop thinking that way or you'll have me to deal with."

Sam smiled. "Yes, boss."

CHAPTER 2

"This is what we've been waiting years for, Adam. We've set the wheels in motion; it's my intention to keep that momentum going. That bitch hasn't known what's hit her since the attack. You did a good job, knifing that fella of hers, injuring him just enough for it to make a difference."

"Thanks, Dad. I thought you were going to give me a bollocking when we heard he was out for the count for days."

"Nah, I'm proud of you. If anything, it's given us the time we needed to put the finishing touches to our plan, or should I say, make a few much-needed amendments."

"It has? What's next for us?"

"Today, we up the ante and get that bitch and her team to start taking us seriously. At this time, they have no idea we're behind the attack on her fella, but she'll know soon enough."

"I'm so excited. We seemed to have been planning this for a while, and finally it's all starting to slot together."

Ian chinked his pint glass against his son's. "Sup up, we need to set off soon. Our next victim awaits us."

They both laughed and downed the rest of their drinks.

...

Half an hour later, with the night drawing in, they drove out to the large house owned by the woman they had chosen to punish. The victim, Gabriella Addis, lived in an older manor house, out in the country about five miles from Workington. They had been following her movements for the past couple of weeks, learning her routine to ensure their plan would go smoothly once it was initiated.

The house went dark downstairs as the final light in the lounge was switched off. Ian had gained access to the property the week before when he'd pretended to be a workman checking the plumbing in the area. Gabby had foolishly left him alone in the kitchen, giving him the time to steal one of the spare keys dangling from the keyring in the back door. It always puzzled him why people did that, instead of keeping the spare keys elsewhere in the property.

Damn idiots. Most of them have shit for brains these days.

"Are you ready for this?"

Adam nodded. "Let's do this, Dad. Our first venture together. I'm so excited."

"Keep your excitement in check, son, I know you won't let me down. Just remember what I told you: stay calm, don't get flustered, and we'll pull this off with ease. We've got this. Don't forget, these women deserve everything that's coming to them."

Adam high-fived his father. "Don't worry, I won't mess it up, I promise. I did that psychiatrist good and proper, didn't I? I showed you how ready I am for this."

He slapped a hand on his son's back. "You definitely did that. Right, let's get in there. We're going to need to stick to the grass, avoid the gravel crunching under our feet. There's no dog in the house, that's her second mistake. These women will never learn to take their safety seriously."

"Yeah, she ain't got no form of security going on either, that's another nail in her coffin, ain't it?"

Ian raised his thumb. "Now you're thinking like me. She's been her own worst enemy for too long, it's time for it to bite her in the arse. I'm going to enjoy this."

Their van was parked a little way down the road, tucked behind a huge hedge, just in case a motorist drove by and thought it was suspicious. Ian carried his bag of equipment to the rear of the property. He stood still and waited for the light to go out in the bathroom above them. Approaching the back door, he slipped his hand through the cat flap.

Why the heck do people install these? They're just asking for trouble!

The key was still in the lock. He removed it, allowing himself to use the spare key he'd stolen. He placed a finger to his lips and then led the way into the vast kitchen. He'd admired the grandeur of the house when he'd visited the week before, now he couldn't care less about it. All he was interested in was getting upstairs and dealing with the woman.

"When we reach the stairs, remember what I told you: older houses tend to creak more; stick to the edges, there's less chance of attracting attention that way."

"Got it."

Ian led the way through the kitchen and into the grand hallway, the main feature being the sweeping mahogany staircase. The moonlight filtering through the large window situated on the half-landing was all they needed to guide them up the stairs, without having any mishaps. At the top, Ian paused to get his bearings, his gaze drawn to the sliver of light showing under the door at the end of the hallway. He knew they'd need to pass the other five bedrooms to get to it. Again, he instructed his son to keep to the edge, sliding against the walls if necessary.

Once they had reached the other end of the landing, Ian paused to listen. The woman was humming. The floorboards creaking now and again on the other side of the door told him she hadn't made it into bed yet. They would need to bide their time until she dived under the quilt. He suspected there would be less chance of her putting up a fight if she was settled in bed. Suddenly, all went quiet inside the room, except for the movement of the bed he picked up when he strained his ear. He raised a thumb, giving his son the go-ahead, then entered the room.

"Scream and we'll kill your son," he warned with a pointed finger aimed at her.

Gabby's mouth dropped open. She clutched the quilt in front of her, drawing the flower- patterned material around her chest. After a few seconds, as it dawned on her what was happening, she asked, "What do you want? I haven't got any money, not here in the house."

Adam and Ian stepped into the room and closed the door behind them.

"We don't want your money. We want you."

Gabby opened her mouth to scream, and Ian wagged his finger.

"Don't do it, I'm not one for making idle threats."

"Please, don't hurt me. My son is only five, he needs me in his life."

"Does he? How much time do you spend with him during the course of the day? And I'm not talking about the weekends."

"Enough. I work full-time. He's taken care of. He's not neglected. Why are you asking me this? It's as if you're accusing me of abandoning my child when nothing could be further from the truth. I love him, he's my world. Everything I do is for him and his well-being."

"Ha, who are you trying to kid, lady? That child deserves

more of your time, not less of it, just because you have a thriving business. You need to be at home, caring for him."

"That's an old-fashioned view you have. Times have changed. Women can have it all now, a career and a family."

"Whatever, my views are different to yours. At the end of the day, it's the kids who suffer. You're just too wrapped up in your own world to realise that. Anyway, who gives a toss what you think? We're here to show you the error of your ways."

She frowned, her gaze flicking between them. "What are you talking about?"

"You'll find out soon enough."

Ian and his son approached the bed. She shuffled back against the headboard and clutched the quilt tighter in her trembling hands. Adam tugged the end of the cover, and a battle for the fabric ensued until Adam's strength overpowered hers.

Then Gabby was exposed, dressed in a silky pyjama suit that consisted of the briefest of shorts and the flimsiest of tops. Ian's trousers bulged, but he ignored his sexual urges; he wasn't here for that, although seeing what was on offer, his mind wavered for a few moments.

"Please, don't hurt me. I have money, lots of it, but I don't keep it here, in the house. I can make a deal with you. I'll get you what you need within forty-eight hours if you walk away now, leave me and my son alone."

Ian tipped his head back and laughed, not caring if he woke Tyler or not. "We ain't about to bargain with you. Our plan is set in stone, and we intend seeing it through to the satisfying conclusion," he shouted.

"Please, keep your voice down, you'll wake my son. He doesn't need to be a part of this. I'm begging you to keep him out of whatever you have in store for me." She ran a hand over her colourless cheeks.

"Carry on begging. It ain't gonna make an ounce of difference to what happens to you." His gaze drifted to the packet of pills lying on her bedside table. "Take sleepers, do ya?"

"Now and again. I haven't taken any tonight."

"Not yet." He laughed again.

"Mummy, Mummy," her child shouted in the hallway outside the bedroom.

"Get him before he tries to make a run for it," Ian ordered.

Adam bolted for the door, yanked it open and grabbed the terrified child by the scruff. "What do you want me to do with him?"

"Put him in the chair. Take his top off and use it to tie him to the chair."

"Mummy, Mummy, help me," little Tyler screeched.

Gabby tried to make her escape, to rescue her son, but Ian latched on to her wrist and ankle and pinned her to the bed.

"Don't even think about getting off this bed." He tightened his grip on her wrist and ankle until she cried out in pain.

"You're hurting me! There's no need for this. I'm willing to do anything you want me to do, just please, don't hurt us. It's okay, Tyler, do as the men say, honey."

"Mummy, I'm scared. Who are they?"

"Just someone Mummy knows. Sit very still; they're only playing a game with us. Be brave, little one. All this will be over soon."

Ian stared at her and then laughed. "Too right it'll be over, but not until we've had our fun. If I let you go, are you gonna promise to behave yourself? Have we got an understanding now?"

"Yes. I promise. Don't hurt Tyler. If you have to hurt me, then so be it, but don't hurt my boy. He has done nothing wrong. He's five, for Christ's sake."

"We know how old he is. Stop treating me as if I'm stupid

—I'm not. We're not. We've been planning all of this for months. You don't even recognise me, do you?"

She stared at him, her eyes narrowing as she thought. "No, I've never seen you before. This must be a mistake, you've obviously got the wrong house, the wrong family. Leave now, without harming us, and I swear I won't go to the police."

"You won't get the chance to go to the police," he sneered and leaned over her. He glanced up, then walked around the bed, picked up the tablets, popped them out of the strip and offered them to her, along with a glass of water. "Take them, all of them."

"What? I can't. If I took them all, they'd kill me."

His lips parted into a wide grin. "By Jove, I believe she's got it, at last. I told you to swallow them. Do it now or I'll make your son take them instead. The choice is yours."

Gabby looked over at her son, tears dripping onto her cheeks in a steady stream. "Forgive me, Tyler. I want you to always remember that I love you."

"Yada, yada, enough of the theatrics. Take the damn tablets and let's get on with things."

"And if I do as you ask, what then?" Gabby's voice caught in her throat.

"You'll see, won't you? Do it. I'll give you to the count of five before I march over there and ram them down Tyler's gullet."

"Mummy!" Tyler screamed. He sobbed and tried to kick out at Adam as he finished tying him to the chair. "Get away from me. I don't like this game. I don't want to play with you. I hate you! You're a bad man."

Adam chuckled and put his head close to Tyler's. "You better believe it, son. Now keep that mouth of yours shut or we're going to do even worse things to your mummy, got that?"

Tyler switched his gaze to his mother, as if seeking her approval or advice.

"It's okay, sweetheart. Just do as they say. Mummy's here. We'll get through this together and then we'll have a nice bowl of ice cream."

"Oh yes, let's do that, I'll have chocolate sauce on mine, too," Adam quipped. He tickled Tyler in the ribs.

"Get off me. I hate chocolate sauce. I don't want any ice cream, all I want is my mummy."

"You've got yourself a right little mummy's boy there, haven't you?" Ian asked. "It's a shame you won't be around to watch him grow up. I want to assure you, we're gonna take good care of him when you're gone. Stop messing me about and take the damn tablets." He took one step towards Tyler.

"I'll do it. I'm not good at taking tablets, it's going to take me a while to get them down. I'm going to need more water than I've got there."

"Adam, get another glass from downstairs and fill it with water." His son ran out of the room, his footsteps sounding in the hallway and on the stairs until they reached the ground floor. Seconds later, he returned. He entered the room and thrust the glass into Gabby's hand.

Ian gave her the tablets, three at a time. Gabby made a fuss of swallowing them. She coughed, but Ian ignored her dramatics and forced her to take the others he held in the palm of his sweaty hand.

"You've got two minutes before I make Tyler have the rest. Now, get them down your neck."

"I can't, they're not going down, they're lodged in my throat. I'm not used to taking this many, I only usually have one at a time. Don't make me have any more, please."

Ian pulled a face and then mimicked her whining. "The clock is ticking. Do it or… I'll carry out my threat and see if

Tyler can be more obliging when both your lives are at risk. We'll see if he's as brave as he thinks he is."

"No, I'll do it. Don't hurt my son. Give them to me."

Ian tipped the rest of the pills into her open palm, and Gabby stared at them for a few seconds, gulped nosily, and then threw them into her mouth. Ian offered her the glass of water. She closed her eyes and tipped her head back. Then spluttered, as if she was choking on the pills.

"Don't you dare spit them out. Swallow them, bitch. Stop taking me for a fool. I'm warning you, spit them out and they go straight in the kid's mouth. That's a promise not a threat."

Gabby's eyes widened as her fear escalated. The lump in her throat disappeared. Her mouth opened, showing him that she had swallowed them.

"What now? Are you going to rape me?"

"I wouldn't want to dip my wick in there, grant me with some sense. You might think you're something special, but you ain't. I'm particular about who I have sex with, and as far as I'm concerned, you'd be the last in the queue."

Gabby let out a relieved sigh. "Then what are you going to do with me?"

He noticed that her words were beginning to slur, and she was swaying from side to side as the tablets took effect. He returned to the other side of the bed and picked up his bag. He opened it and removed a pack of blades.

"You're gonna slit your wrists."

She gasped, terrified, and shook her head. Her gaze shot over to her son who was crying out for her. "No, I can't do it. Don't make me do this, not in front of Tyler."

"Shut up! You'll do as you're told. How many times do I have to repeat myself, bitch?"

Tears emerged, and her head lolled to the side. "I can't. I won't," she slurred. "Tyler, I love you."

"I love you, Mummy. Why are these men doing this? I

want to cuddle you. Tell you everything is going to be okay, but I can't…"

"It's oka… son… mummmmmy's goin' to be okay."

Ian shook her shoulders. "Don't you pass out on me. We still have work to do." He rammed the blade in her hand, knowing she was in no fit state to lash out at him.

"Mummy, Mummy… what's the matter with you?"

"It's all righ… Tyle…"

Gabby's head lurched to the side, and Ian had to hold her upright to prevent her from toppling over.

"Oh no you don't. Come back here. Do it, or I'll cut Tyler's throat."

The boy screamed, and Gabby tried to fight the tiredness threatening to overwhelm her.

"Give it to me."

Ian placed the blade between her finger and thumb and guided her hand over her left wrist. "I'm happy to help you. Here's the vein, cut it there."

Gabby sobbed and let go of the blade. "I don't wa…nt to. Don't do this to me. I don't wa…nt to die." Snot mixed with her tears, her eyes barely open now.

Ian picked up the blade and yelled in her face, "You're beginning to piss me off. Either you do what I say, or I'll kill your son in front of you. This is your final warning."

Gabby's head rolled from the left to the right in slow motion. She opened her eyes to look at her son and sobbed harder. "Tyl… I lov… you."

Tyler howled and then shrieked, "Mummy, don't do it. I love you… too…"

Ian put the blade between her thumb and finger again and directed it over the prominent vein in her wrist. This time, the blade met her skin and cut her flesh. Gabby no longer had the strength to object or scream. She just stared at the blood dripping onto her bedding.

Her eyes flickered shut, and she rested her head on Ian's shoulder.

Tyler was shouting and crying intermittently for his mother until Adam slapped his hand over the child's mouth.

Ian checked Gabby's pulse—it was weak. "She's going. I need to get her moved. Leave the kid and help me."

Adam rushed to assist his father. They dragged Gabby off the bed, hooked each of her arms over their shoulders and eased her towards the window.

"No, leave my mummy… leave her alone," Tyler screeched, his heart clearly breaking.

"Hold her upright," Ian ordered.

Adam took the strain and hooked his arms around Gabby's waist. Ian unlocked the sash window and raised the bottom one.

"Nooooooo, Mummy… I want… my mummy."

"Shut up," Ian shouted.

He took hold of Gabby's right arm while Adam supported her left one, and they pushed her head out of the window, then they both reached for one of her legs.

"Ready?"

"Yep."

"Let her go."

Ian grinned and watched the woman's body hit the gravel beneath the window with a thump. Tyler was inconsolable, and his screams became high-pitched.

Adam rushed back to the boy. He tried to silence the child. "Hush, it's all right. You're coming home with us."

"I don't want to." Tyler sniffled, his chest rising and falling as he struggled to find his breath.

Adam untied him only for Tyler to kick out and hit him with his fists.

"Leave me alone… Mummy, where's my mummy?"

"She's gone. You're ours now. You're going to live with us.

We'll treat you right, you'll see." Adam tried to fend off the attack without hurting the child.

Ian came closer and swiped a hand around Tyler's face. The action successfully shut the child up but only for a few seconds. Eventually, Tyler's commotion got far worse, driving them both crazy.

"Get something to shut the kid up, for fuck's sake. I'm sick of him already. Either that or he joins his mother."

"You can't do that, Dad. He's just seen his mother get murdered. You'd be cut up if that happened to you, wouldn't you?"

"I've got news for you, it did happen to me and it didn't bother me one iota."

Adam's eyes widened at the shocking news. He stood and searched his father's bag of equipment and found a roll of gaffer tape. He tore a strip off and stuck it over Tyler's mouth, but not before Ian had to lend a hand keeping the child still.

"Peace at last. Let's get him out of here."

"We should take some of his clothes and toys with us."

Ian contemplated his son's suggestion for a moment or two. "Yes, okay, you're right. Make it snappy, we need to get going. There's a roll of black bags in the holdall."

Adam swiftly tore off one of the bags and left the room. Ian towered over the little boy, intimidating him into keeping quiet, not that the tape covering his mouth wasn't already doing that job. His mind wandered back to when he was a kid. The torment he'd felt when his mother refused to give him a spare second of her time. After several fraught images entered his mind, he shook his head and returned to the present and the urgent job in hand: getting out of the house. But first, he was determined to search Gabby's room, see what he could find to sell, which would help towards the cost of raising her kid until he was in his late teens.

He tore off a black bag and immediately made his way over to the large jewellery box sitting on the dressing table. He checked the contents and whistled. "Wow, this should do nicely, Raymondo will be rubbing his hands when he sets his eyes on this lot."

Tyler fidgeted in the chair and tried to speak behind the tape.

Ian glanced his way, held up one of his mother's diamond necklaces and grinned. "Why all the fuss? We're talking about your future here, or more to the point, funding it. Yes, I'm not messing about, standing here sifting through it, I'll just take the lot and see what we can get for it. If you're a very good boy, I might even let you keep a small item to remember her by."

He laughed, and Tyler just stared at him.

Adam entered the room moments later, his sack as full as Santa's as he set off from the North Pole on Christmas Eve.

"Jesus, lucky he's travelling light," Ian joked. "Okay, I'll carry the bag, you untie the kid, and we'll get out of here."

Adam untied Tyler, and the boy immediately tried to escape. Adam had to use force to get him to behave. Ten minutes later, they eventually made it to the van parked down the road.

CHAPTER 3

*S*am was up with the birds the following morning. Before she even considered getting out of bed, she rang the hospital to check on Rhys and was informed that he'd had a good night and was still sleeping. She told the nurse that she'd call in to see him at the end of her shift, then she jumped in the shower, put on her leisure suit and took Sonny and Casper for a walk around the nearby park.

After Crystal and Vernon had left the previous evening, she had visited Doreen and apprised her of the situation with Rhys. Her neighbour was sympathetic and reiterated that if Sam needed her to look after both dogs in the immediate future, she was more than willing to care for them.

So, it had been arranged that Sam would get up half an hour earlier to take the dogs for their walk. She would then drop them off at Doreen's, and Vernon would pick them up at around one to take them for a long walk around the lake, then he would return them to Doreen once more.

She felt blessed to have such good people around her, especially as Rhys' parents still hadn't intimated they were having a change of heart about visiting him.

Dogs walked and dropped off as planned, Sam got ready for work, and at ten minutes to nine, she arrived at the station and parked in her allocated space. Bob drew up alongside her seconds later.

"Hi, how's it going?" she asked.

"Should you be here today? How's Rhys?"

"Pretty much the same. I checked in with the nurses earlier, and they told me he'd had a reasonable night, so here I am, back to the grind."

"You're nuts. You should make the most of it and take some time off, not be here with us."

"Anyone would think you're trying to keep me away, partner. You haven't been telling me porkies about being on top of the paperwork, have you?"

He pulled a face and slapped a hand over his chest. "Would I?"

Sam sighed and rolled her eyes. "I refuse to answer that until I see the evidence for myself."

He opened the main door to the station and gestured for her to go first. Standing in the reception area, desk sergeant Nick Travis was talking with someone on the phone, his brow heavily knitted together.

"Everything all right, Nick?" she whispered.

He raised a finger and told the caller he would sort it out and get back to them ASAP.

"Sorry about that, ma'am. I'm glad you're here, good to see you again. I take it your fella is on the mend now?"

"He is, but I think I'll be better off here, searching for his attacker, rather than continue to sit by his bedside, going out of my mind. What was that all about, Nick?"

"We received an urgent call around twenty minutes ago from a foreign lady needing assistance. I sent a couple of my men out to the house to investigate what was going on. They've just got back to me, told me the woman is beside herself and that they could do with an interpreter; she's Spanish. The problem is, I'm not sure we have anyone we can call on to help." He peered at his watch. "I can try and contact someone just after nine, see if an interpreter can attend the scene, but that could take hours to arrange."

Sam mulled over the dilemma and clicked her finger and thumb together. "Hang fire on that, I seem to remember Suzanna telling me that she'd attended evening classes to learn a language a few years ago. I'm sure she said it was a Spanish class she joined."

"That'd be great if she did. She's not here yet, at least, I can't recall seeing her arrive."

Bob opened the door again and checked the car park. "Nope, her usual space is empty. Do you want me to give her a call?"

"If you wouldn't mind?" Nick replied.

Bob removed his phone from his pocket and glanced up. "No need, she's here now. I'll ask her to get a move on." He shot out of the front door before Sam could stop him.

"He's an eager beaver when he wants to be. Do you need me to attend the scene?"

Nick smiled. "I was hoping you'd volunteer. I didn't want to put the burden on you, what with you only just back on duty."

"Jot down the address, and the three of us will take a drive out there."

He smiled and handed her a piece of paper. "Already sorted for you."

Sam took the paper and studied the address. "Camerton? Yes, I know it. Okay, we'll set off now. See you later."

She left the station and gestured for Suzanna and Bob to turn around. "We're heading over to the scene."

"What? All of us?" Bob asked, surprised.

"Yes, Bob. Do you have a problem with that?"

He turned to walk towards Sam's car. "Yours or mine? And no, I don't have a problem with it."

"This is all very exciting," Suzanna said. "I can't promise I'll be much use, boss. My Spanish is rusty as hell, but I'm willing to give it a go."

"We'll muddle through together. I learnt French at school and have used it a few times on holidays to France ever since. They say if you know one of the popular foreign languages, you can pretty much communicate in five or six others."

"I wish. We'll soon find out. Any idea what this is all about, boss?" Suzanna asked.

The three of them got in the car, and Sam shook her head. "No idea. Nick was kind of flustered when we arrived. The address is out in Camerton, though. Can't think of too many houses out that way, can you, Bob?"

"No, I can't. Want me to put the info into the satnav, or are you okay?"

"Yes, do it. The house might be tricky to find once we reach the other end." Sam switched on the engine and reversed out of the space.

"All sorted. It's right out in the sticks, no other houses around, according to the map."

It took approximately ten minutes to reach the house. A patrol car with two uniformed officers was already at the scene. Sam had not long arrived when Des Markham, the local pathologist, pulled up with his team.

Sam, Bob and Suzanna got out of the car, eager to find out what was going on. The uniformed officers recognised Sam, and the older of the two approached them. His colleague remained behind, chatting to the distraught lady.

"What's going on?" Sam asked once the officer was in earshot.

"We arrived to find the woman crying, sobbing, frantic she was. She managed to call nine-nine-nine and just about gave the operator enough information regarding her location. When we got here, she pleaded with us to follow her. There's a dead woman around there; the bedroom window above was open. Looks like a jumper to us, ma'am. But we can't get anything else out of the woman. We're assuming she's the cleaner and had shown up for work; presumably she discovered the body a little while later."

"Ah, right, that makes sense. Suzanna, do you want to try and get some more information out of her? No pressure."

"Not much." Suzanna laughed, and the officer escorted her around the side of the house.

"What have we got here?" Des joined them and asked.

"We're not too sure yet. Apparently, there's a body around the back. We've yet to venture around there. A member of my team is trying to get further information out of the woman who found her before we take a look."

"Well, that might work for you, Detective, but time is of the essence for me and my team." He marched off.

Sam and Bob followed him and one of his technicians.

Des asked Suzanna to remove the witness from the scene, so he could gain access to the deceased. He raised his head and said, "Don't come any closer without a suit on."

"We weren't," Sam assured him. "What have you got?"

"A dead woman, obviously. She has wounds to both wrists. I'm assuming she slit her wrists before she threw herself out of the window."

"Not nice. No wonder the cleaner is upset. We'll see what Suzanna has managed to get out of her and come back to you afterwards."

"As you wish."

"Charming as ever, I see," Bob quipped as they walked away.

"It's still quite early, I suppose we have to factor that in."

"He's still a grouchy old so-and-so at times," Bob mumbled.

"We're all in the same boat, showing up at the scene at the same time. In fairness to him, he's usually the first one on site, and no, that's not me making excuses for him."

"Whatever, I just believe there are better ways of talking to people."

Sam frowned. "That was mild, compared to normal. What's eating you, Bob?"

"Nothing. Okay, I've obviously spoken out of turn, ignore me."

She sniggered. "I intend to."

Bob was usually a little out of sorts on her first morning back to work. Generally, she put his mood down to stress.

Suzanna saw them walking towards her and patted her hand on the woman's arm, then she spoke to the male officer next to her who led the woman away.

"How did it go?" Sam asked.

"She's understandably upset. I think I got the gist of what she was saying, but if we can get a professional to confirm it, I'd feel much better."

"We'll sort that out later. Go on."

"She told me she arrived at eight-fifteen, her usual time. She let herself into the house, and it was quiet, too quiet. She saw Gabby Addis' car was still on the drive. She called out and when she got no response, she collected her cleaning stuff from the kitchen and went upstairs. She always likes to start in the main bedroom. The door was closed. She knocked on it but didn't receive an answer, so she opened the door, and her eye was immediately drawn to the window which was open. She thought that was unusual; Miss Addis isn't usually one for leaving a window open if she leaves the property. She called out for her, thinking she might be in the en suite, but the room was empty. That's when she went to investigate the window. She looked down and saw Gabby Addis' body. She ran downstairs to see if Gabby was okay."

"It must have been quite a shock for her. Does Addis have a partner?"

"I tried to ask, but I don't think she understood me. Then she started sobbing and saying the name Tyler over and over. I tried to get out of her who that was, and she kept putting her arm out to the side, at the same level as her hip."

"Could she be talking about a child?" Bob asked.

"Jesus, yes. I bet that's what she meant. Thanks, Suzanna. Why don't we all put on a protective suit and see what we can find in the house?"

Suzanna and Bob both agreed, and the three of them made their way back to the vehicle. Sam handed out the last of her suits and made a mental note to stock up when they returned to the station. Out of courtesy, she let Des know what was going on. He granted them permission to enter the house with the understanding that they report their findings to him once they were finished.

Sam led the way. They didn't bother checking downstairs. Instead, they went upstairs to search the other bedrooms. It wasn't long before they found a child's bedroom. On the bedside table was a picture of a young boy, aged no more than five or six, cuddling the deceased woman.

"Shit. Okay, so she did have a child. We need to find out if the child stayed elsewhere overnight." Sam rotated on the spot to scan the rest of the room. "Seems to me like the boy left in a hurry; the wardrobe doors and some of his drawers are open. The bed has also been slept in."

"Hmm… what if we're talking about a custody battle here? Maybe the ex showed up, took the boy, and the mother couldn't handle it, decided to take her own life."

Sam faced her partner. "It's a possible scenario. That's got to be our first job, see what background information we can dig up. I don't think we can rely on the cleaner to fill in the gaps for us. Did she say how often she comes to the house, Suzanna?"

"Twice a week."

Sam scratched her head. "In that case, we'll need to see if Des can give us an approximate time of death for the woman. I'm going to check the main bedroom, see if there's any kind of disturbance in there." She walked the length of the hallway and entered the vast bedroom. "This is beautiful. Wait, there's blood on the bedding. I'm presuming she slit her wrists on the bed and then moved to the window."

Bob bent down to pick something up in his gloved hand. "Tablets. Maybe she thought about ending her life, found she didn't have enough pills at her disposal and decided to make sure by cutting her wrists."

"What? Then to make absolutely sure, she decided to jump out of the window?" Sam was dubious as to whether that was a reasonable conjecture or not.

"Who knows? I suppose we're going to have to see what Des comes up with during the PM."

"I agree. For now, we need to get the lowdown on the family dynamics and go from there. I wonder if that's why the cleaner is upset. Obviously seeing her employer lying splat on the gravel will have disturbed her, but what if she's distraught because the boy has gone missing?"

"I think that's a given," Bob said. "I'm going to see what Google can tell us."

"Good call." Sam wandered around the room and poked her head into the en suite.

"What about a jewellery box?" Suzanna asked. "I can't see one."

"Check the drawers over that side, will you, Suzanna? I'll have a root around in the wardrobe. She might be someone who prefers to keep that sort of thing hidden, rather than on show." Sam slid back the mirrored door at one end and began her search. "Nothing here." After searching high and low through the rest of the wardrobe, she moved around the room, peering behind the couple of pictures hanging on the walls. "No sign of a safe either. It's a huge house for just the two of them."

"That's an understatement, it's ginormous," Bob said. "Okay, I've located several articles about her. According to this, she runs a successful recruitment agency, one of the best in the whole of the north of England."

"Interesting. Maybe she had financial worries and decided to take her own life, but then, that wouldn't account for her son going missing. How recent was the article, Bob?"

"A few weeks ago. Could a business take a downturn like that overnight? Perhaps she spouted her mouth off before the taxman got his cut and HMRC left her broke."

"Possibly. We won't know for sure until we delve into her bank statements. Either way, there's no jewellery to be found here. Suzanna, any luck over that side of the room?"

"Nothing whatsoever, boss."

"Okay, let's check out the rest of the rooms upstairs and then have a quick scout around downstairs. Did the cleaner say if the doors were open when she arrived?"

Suzanna shook her head. "She didn't mention it and, to be honest, I forgot to ask."

"No problem, we can revisit that when we see her again."

They split up and searched the other three bedrooms and met up on the landing again.

"Nothing else to see up here," Bob confirmed.

"Likewise," Sam said.

The three of them made their way down the grand sweeping staircase and entered the large lounge. The room was tastefully decorated with white walls. The pops of colour in the cushions and the soft furnishings were a contrast to the starkness. Again, Sam checked behind the various paintings on the walls in the hope of finding a safe. She found nothing. The downstairs was tidy, not much to be seen in the lounge or in the office next door. They entered the kitchen, which again took Sam's breath away. She noticed the back door on the right and walked towards it.

"There's no sign of broken glass anywhere that I can see and no key in the lock here." She tried the handle with her gloved hand, and the door opened. "That's interesting. I'll get the techs to dust for prints, just in case."

"Where else should we look? Outside? There might be a garage or gym, possibly an annexe in the grounds."

"Worth a shout. Can you deal with that, Bob?"

"On it now." He left the house via the back door.

Sam walked around the long kitchen island and checked the sink. It was clear, no dirty dishes or even a glass or two in there to give them any leads to go on. "Maybe the ex had a key for the back door," she muttered, thinking out loud.

"Possibly," Suzanna agreed.

Sam and Suzanna left the house.

"Can you ask the woman... sorry, what was her name?"

"Maria Garcia."

"Ask her if she has a contact number for a member of Gabby's family, perhaps her mother or father."

Suzanna ambled over to the woman, who was still sobbing and wiping her nose on a tissue, while Sam took in her surroundings. The manor house was set in its own grounds. A huge hedge, maybe eight to ten feet tall, blocked the view of the road to the front. At the rear was a small wooded area beyond the large expanse of neatly cut striped lawn.

Could the child be in the woods? Hiding from someone? His father or an intruder? Is this a suicide, or was Gabby killed? So many questions and, at this stage, very few answers or leads to steer the investigation in the right direction or even get it started.

Bob's voice startled her. "Nothing else out here. The garage is full of junk, probably why her car is parked on the drive."

"You scared the shit out of me. I wish you'd cough or something to let me know you're around, rather than sneak up on me."

"I hardly crept up on you, the noise of the gravel would have woken the dead."

"You're unbelievable. How can you say that, given the circumstances?"

He cringed. "Sorry, opened my mouth, as usual, before I engaged my brain."

"You said it."

Suzanna joined them to report back. "Maria's not sure. She thinks her parents live locally but has no idea of either their address or phone number."

"Hmm… maybe we should recheck the house, search for Gabby's phone. I don't recall seeing it, do you?"

Bob and Suzanna both shook their heads.

"I'll nip back in, if you want me to?" Bob suggested.

"Yes, okay. You do that. Suzanna and I will check if Des has any news for us."

Bob entered via the back doorway. Sam and Suzanna returned to the crime scene. Des was standing a few feet away from the deceased's body while a member of his team took photos from different angles.

"Have you come to any conclusions yet?" Sam asked.

"Not really."

"How about a time of death?"

"Judging by the amount of lividity, I would hazard a guess that she died sometime last night, possibly between the hours of ten and midnight. I can't be more accurate than that, I'm afraid. What about you? Anything?"

"We've learnt that the woman had a child. We've searched the house, can't find him in the property."

"Strange. Any sign of a break-in?"

"No, the back door was unlocked, no key in it. If you can get one of your men to dust it for prints. I touched it but had gloves on. Not sure if Maria, the cleaner, touched it or not."

"We'll get a sample of her prints so we can dismiss them. I must get on, we've just had another call about a pile-up on the A595, two fatalities at the scene. Looks like I'm in for a busy day."

"I feel for you. I promise not to pester you for the results for this one." She grinned.

"But you're going to anyway, I can see it in your eyes. You'll get them as soon as I've had the chance to type them up. Is that good enough for you?"

"It is, thanks. Umm… one last question, are we dealing with a suicide or murder here?"

"Hard to tell, is my honest answer. I must get on, and yes, I will carry out the necessary tests to obtain that precise information for you. Now, if you'll excuse me."

Sam took a step back and peered over her shoulder at the sound of crunching gravel behind her. "Anything?"

"No phone, not from what I could see in there. Maybe the kid took it when he ran off."

"*If* he ran off." Sam's eye was drawn to the woods again. "We need to get some extra bodies out here to search the woodland. I won't be able to rest knowing that the boy might be hiding out there."

"I'll sort it."

"No, let Suzanna place the call. I need you to bring up that article again for me."

Suzanna took a few steps and rang the station. Bob flicked through his tabs and offered Sam his phone for her to read the moderately long article.

"Good job I can speed-read."

"One of your many talents," Bob replied. "What are you searching for? Anything in particular?"

"I'm wondering if she mentioned her parents, or possibly a name of a friend who has been instrumental in helping her to gain her achievements. It'll save the team a bit of time sourcing the information."

"There's a reason you're an inspector." Bob chuckled.

Sam laughed and shook her head. "Let's see what we have here. Ah, yes, halfway down she gives credit to both her parents, Sheila and Roland Addis, who are both lecturers at the Cumbria University in Carlisle. We need to get in touch with them, see if they live locally. If not, we're going to need to take a trip up there to visit them at some point during the day, the sooner the better."

Bob held out his hand for his phone. Sam handed it back to him, and he rang the station.

"Hi, Claire, can you get an address for us, please? It's for the deceased's parents, Sheila and Roland Addis, they're lecturers at Cumbria University in Carlisle. We're not sure if they travel every day to work or what, but it would be good to find out… Yep, I'll hold." Bob tapped his foot as he waited.

Suzanna ended her call and came to stand alongside Sam. "Two more patrols are on their way out here, boss."

"Good, thanks. The problem we have now is what to do with Maria. We're going to need to get a statement from her ASAP."

"I can get that arranged, if you want?"

"Yes, you do that. Depending on what Bob comes up with,

we'll get back to the station soon. Maria will need a lift home. Can you have a word with the officers dealing with her at the moment?"

Suzanna nodded and walked off.

"That's great. Cheers, Claire, we'll call at the house, see if anyone is at home." Bob went to hang up, but Sam asked to speak to Claire.

"Hi, it's me. We need to get the ball rolling on the background checks, Claire. Can you and the team get started for us? We've discovered a recent article about the woman in *The Independent*. Have a quick read of it, it's got the name of her business for me. We'll call round there after we've spoken to the next of kin. They remain our priority for now. We're going to need access to Gabby Addis' bank accounts, and can you also try and find out who her ex-partner would have been? According to the cleaner, who found the deceased's body, she has a child called Tyler, possibly between the ages of five and six; he's missing from the property. We've got patrols on the way out here. They'll be conducting a search of the area. There are no immediate neighbours, so no point in us carrying out a house-to-house. I think I've covered everything."

"I've made notes, boss. I'll get the team working on all you've requested. Hopefully we'll have something positive to tell you upon your return."

"Here's hoping, Claire. See you later." Sam handed the phone back to Bob.

"I've checked where the parents' house is, it's out at Wigton."

"A tad too far to take a punt they'll be there during the day. Let's give the uni a call instead, see if they've got any lectures today."

"On it now."

Sam paced the area, the gravel moving and crunching noisily under her feet until Bob ended the call.

"The wife is at the uni, and the husband has taken the day off. The secretary wouldn't give me any further information. Not sure if that was intentional or because she simply didn't know."

"Okay, let's get over there, see if he's in."

CHAPTER 4

Thirty minutes later, with the flow of traffic on their side, Sam and Bob drew up outside the Addis' detached home. It was one of four comparatively new properties situated in a select cul-de-sac. They'd left Suzanna back at the scene; it had been decided she would oversee the search for the boy in their absence.

"Nice pad. Still, I suppose with two lecturers in the house, they can afford a gaff this size," Bob stated.

"It is nice. I think I'd prefer their daughter's isolated house rather than other houses being in close proximately like these."

Bob raised an eyebrow. "Yeah, and look where that isolation got her."

They exited the car and walked up the pretty coloured pathway. The beds on either side of it were full of summer plants in varying sizes.

"I hear you. Let's hope the father is in. It's not looking hopeful with no car on the drive."

"He might have tucked it away in the garage."

"True enough. There's only one way of finding out." Sam

rang the doorbell. A yappy dog barked inside but was promptly shouted at to be quiet.

A man in his late fifties to sixties opened the door. He eyed them with caution. "Hello, can I help?"

"Sorry to trouble you, Mr Addis. I'm DI Sam Cobbs, and this is my partner, DS Bob Jones. We're from the Cumbria Constabulary out in Workington. I wondered if it would be possible to have a word with you."

"I see. Do I have to ask what this is about, or are you going to tell me?"

"May we come in?"

"If you insist. I have an appointment with my optometrist in an hour, so you'll need to make this quick. Let me put Brady in the kitchen. Come on, boy, in you go."

"We won't keep you too long, sir. It is an urgent matter."

He returned from the end of the hallway and entered the room on the right, expecting them to follow him. The entrance hall was tastefully decorated in a light grey, panelling a key feature, giving it a homely feel that also added a touch of grandeur.

"Come in, take a seat."

Roland chose to sit in one of the brown leather armchairs and gestured for Sam and Bob to take the couch.

"Thank you for agreeing to see us at short notice. I'm afraid I have some bad news for you."

He sat on the edge of his seat, his hands linked together. "What news? Is this about my wife? She was okay when she set off for work this morning."

"No, this is about your daughter."

"Gabby, what about her?"

"We were called out to her house this morning by her cleaner. Unfortunately, your daughter's body was found…"

"What? Her body? What are you telling me, that she's dead?" he shouted, his gaze flitting between them.

"Sadly, yes."

"What? How? I can't believe what I'm hearing. My wife and I only spoke to her last night."

"May I ask what time that was?"

"Around eight. She had just bathed Tyler and put him to bed. How did she die?"

"The pathologist's preliminary findings are inconclusive. We'll know more once the PM has been carried out; hopefully, that will take place this afternoon. Although he's already warned us there might be a slight delay as he had been called out to oversee a fatal accident that has just occurred on the A595."

"Oh my God," Roland said and ran a hand through his short, grey hair. "Is this true? How can she be dead? She's only twenty-nine and has everything to live for. How did this happen?"

"As I stated before, we received a call from the cleaner first thing this morning. She found your daughter's body on the gravel beneath her bedroom window, which was open."

He frowned and scratched his temple. "You're not making any sense. What are you telling me, that you believe my daughter took her own life by throwing herself out of the window?"

"It's a possibility we need to consider at this stage. When you spoke with your daughter, did she voice any concerns to you?"

"No. She was excited as she always was. The conversation we held mainly consisted of Gabby telling us about the plans she'd put in place to open a second recruitment agency in the area. She was happy, so full of… life. Oh my, I can't believe what you're telling me. What about Tyler? Where was he? I hope he didn't see his mother, lying there, dead."

"We're not sure where your grandson is. Maria, the cleaner, told us he lived at the house, but that's all we know.

We've got uniformed officers conducting a search of the surrounding area to try and find him."

"He's missing? I need to call my wife. I'm not sure I can handle this news on my own. I know that must seem a silly thing to say, but we do most things together. She'll know what to do for the best because I'm struggling to make any sense of what I'm hearing. At this moment, all I have is this image of my daughter lying dead… it's a vile image that I would rather not have in my head. On top of that, you're also telling me our grandson has gone missing. Did someone break into her house and do this to her? No, don't answer that, I need to ring Sheila, see what she makes of all this."

"Normally, we would tell the parents together, where possible. We rang the uni to see if you were both at work today, with the intention of coming out to see you and your wife together, but the secretary told us that you were off today, hence the reason we're visiting you at home, rather than at the university."

"Thanks for explaining that, but I really need to speak to my wife before you tell me anything else or ask me any further questions." He stood and left the room.

"He's not taking it too well, is he?" Bob whispered once the door closed behind him.

"Let's be fair, how the hell would you react, hearing that kind of news?"

"Okay, there's no need for you to bite my head off. I was only stating facts."

Sam tutted, impatience getting the better of her. "Sorry for snapping. A little compassion wouldn't go amiss now and again, partner."

"I show it all the time. It's not my fault it's often misinterpreted."

Sam rolled her head from side to side, easing the tension mounting in her neck. "You reckon?"

The door opened, preventing Bob from replying.

"My wife is in bits. She wanted to drive back to speak with you, but I told her to stay there overnight. The last thing I want is for her to have an accident and join my daughter in the mortuary."

"I think that's a wise decision."

"She's struggling to comprehend the fact that we won't see Gabby again. She was our only daughter, we adored her. We're so proud of what she'd accomplished at her age, and with a child to care for at the same time, too. Not every woman would have been able to have done that."

"Did she have a partner?"

"Sadly, Marlon died three years ago, around the time her business was just taking off."

"I'm sorry to hear that. How did he die?"

"He had a brain tumour. They were due to tie the knot while he was in hospital, but he deteriorated quickly and was taken from us. He always treated my daughter as though she were a princess. We welcomed him to our family the second we were introduced to him. They were made for each other. They were overjoyed that Gabby fell pregnant before they received Marlon's diagnosis. Talking of which, where do you think Tyler could be?"

"We're not sure if he's run off. To be honest, the scene at the house is a perplexing one for us to understand."

"Perplexing, in what way? Please, don't hold back, I need to know the truth."

"When we searched the main bedroom, we found an empty strip of sleeping tablets. We're presuming Gabby took the tablets. We also discovered that your daughter had cut her wrists on the bed before jumping out of the window."

"That's utter nonsense. My daughter would never kill herself. Why would she when she had everything to live for? A son she loved more than anything in this world, a successful business that was showing no signs of slowing down. It doesn't add up. I can't believe you're sitting here telling me that she's ended her own life. Why would she go to such lengths? It's unthinkable, that's what it is. Hard to fathom, to comprehend, it just doesn't make sense. None of this does. I refuse to accept that she would take her own life."

"Okay, that's given us something to work with. Does she have any other family members living in the area?"

"None, she was an only child. We tried to conceive after we had her but, unfortunately, my wife had a torrid time with the labour; her tubes were badly damaged during the birth. I don't know what the technical term is, but it amounts to the same. We even wasted money on two rounds of IVF, only to be told they hadn't worked."

"I'm so sorry things didn't work out better for you. What about her friends? Did she have anyone close who she could confide in?"

"Yes, Katherine. Gabby went to school with her, and they've remained best friends ever since. I know, now you're going to ask me what her surname is, aren't you? Sorry, I can't remember. She got married a few years ago to a foreign chap, and her surname sounded like gobbledygook when I heard it."

"Don't worry, we'll ask around, see what her work colleagues can tell us."

"Her staff, you mean. She owned the business, she didn't have colleagues," he corrected her, sharply.

"Sorry, yes, that's what I meant, her staff."

"What happens now?" he asked, his chin dipping to his chest as the emotion so obviously swelled within him.

"We're going to need to wait for the results of the PM to come through. You'll be able to see your daughter once the pathologist has completed his work."

"And what will you be doing in the meantime?"

"We'll be digging into your daughter's background, her finances, see if there is anything worth investigating there. We noticed your daughter didn't have any security in place at the house. Is there a reason for that, sir?"

"Neither of us agrees with the intrusion all this new-fangled technology has to offer. It's like Big Brother watching over us. Best if it's avoided, if possible."

"Sadly, without any security evidence to hand for us to sift through, our job will be that much harder out of the starting blocks. The fact that Gabby's house is pretty remote, with no other neighbours nearby, I sense will only end up adding to our frustration."

"I hope not. Is this you getting all your excuses out of the way first, Inspector?"

"Not at all, sir. I'm being totally frank with you. Is there anything you can tell us about your daughter's past that you believe will help with our investigation?"

"Such as? I'm at a loss to even think about anything else, other than her lying there… and my grandson being missing. You have to find him. He's a sweet child, only five. He's led a sheltered life. He won't know what to do if he's out there all alone."

"Do you have a recent photo of him on your phone? Something we can release to the public for help?" She kicked herself for not taking a snap of the photo of Tyler and his mother, sitting on his bedside table, before they had left the house.

"Yes, I took a few recently. We had a fun day out together a couple of months ago. It was such a rarity for us to get the time off together. Gabby is, or should I say was, a workaholic. Don't get me wrong, she didn't neglect her son at all, but her work was always a priority in her life."

"I completely understand. She was trying to look out for

both of them, secure their future without a man being present."

"Yes, that's right."

He found a suitable photo which he forwarded to Sam's number.

"That's great," she replied, once her phone pinged that it had arrived.

He also sent her a picture of his daughter. Gabby had been a stunning lady. Sam could imagine men falling for her beautiful hazel eyes and her fair skin. Her smile was reflected in her eyes and showed nothing but love for her son and family. Sam realised then that there was no way this woman would have contemplated taking her own life. Therefore, going forward, she would be treating this as a murder inquiry. Hopefully, Des would agree with her once he'd performed the PM later that day.

Sam and Bob stayed with Roland for the next hour. He was a willing participant in the interview, answering all of Sam's questions about Gabby's previous careers and any men she'd been involved with during the past ten years, which Sam found welcoming but also unusual to have that level of detail from a father. In Sam's experience, it tended to be the lady of the house who was willing to supply details worth delving into.

"Right, if there's nothing else you can think of, we're going to leave you to it and get started on the investigation."

"Okay. Can you do me a favour first?"

"What's that?"

Roland coughed to clear his throat. "Would you mind checking in with the patrols to see if anyone has found Tyler yet?"

"I can do that for you. We'll see how the rest of the day goes, and if there's still no sign of him by midday tomorrow, I'll call a press conference."

He nodded and offered up a weak smile. "Thank you. I hope you'll have at least had a sighting of him by then. The thought of him being out there alone, at his tender age…" He paused and shuddered. "Well, I really don't want to think about that… if he is alone, just wandering about out there, then I know he's going to be terrified."

Sam quickly rang the station and spoke to Nick. In turn, he radioed the men out on patrol, but the news wasn't what they wanted to hear. No sighting of Tyler yet.

"Don't worry, there was an alert issued earlier. If he's wandering the streets, he'll be spotted and picked up." Again, Sam doubted if this was truly the case, especially as she now suspected they were dealing with a murder inquiry. Her assumption was that if someone had killed Gabby, they had also taken her son.

Roland showed them to the door. "Will you keep my wife and I informed?"

"We will. As soon as there is anything concrete to share with you both. Again, I'm so sorry for your loss."

"Thank you. Will the pathologist get in touch with us when we're able to… see Gabby?"

"Yes, I'll pass on your details to him once we leave here. If Tyler should show up, or if anyone gets in touch with you to do with the investigation, will you contact me?"

"Absolutely. I'll get my appointment out of the way and then travel to Carlisle to speak with my wife. Good luck with the investigation."

"Thank you. I'll be in touch soon."

They left the house, and before they reached the car, Sam had already decided what their next move should be. Up until that point, she'd been struggling to think clearly, wrapped up in Roland's grief.

"Are you okay?" Bob asked.

Sam started the engine. "I am now. We'll head back to the station. I need to make a few calls en route."

"Do you want me to drive?"

"Sounds good to me." She turned the engine off again and slipped out of the car. With Bob now behind the wheel, she said, "Thanks, mate. I'm going to give the hospital a call first, see if Rhys has woken up fully yet, or not."

"It's still a bit early for that, Sam."

"I know. A girl needs to have some hope to cling on to, though." She rang the hospital. As usual, it took a while for the phone to be answered on the ward. "Hi, sorry to trouble you, it's Sam Cobbs here. I was just checking in to see how Rhys has been this morning?"

"Ah, yes. Well, there's no further news I can share with you at this time. He's been asleep most of the morning. Hold on a second, I'll ask my colleague, see if she's got a recent update to share."

The nurse covered the phone, but Sam could still hear them holding a conversation, she just couldn't work out what was being said.

Bob drew up at the next set of traffic lights and asked, "Everything all right?"

"Yeah, they're having a conflab."

The nurse came back on the line. "Hi again, Miss Cobbs, sorry to keep you so long."

"It's no problem, I appreciate how busy you are."

"Thanks for being so understanding. I wish Rhys' brother was as patient as you are."

Sam's heart thudded against her ribs. "Sorry? His brother? Is he there now?"

"No, he was desperate to see him. Once he was given the all-clear, he only ended up sitting with him for five minutes."

"Shit!" Sam mumbled.

"I'm sensing there's a problem, is there?" the nurse asked.

"You could say that. Rhys doesn't have a brother."

"I see, we weren't aware. I'll make a note on the desk not to allow further visitors. All I can do is offer you my sincerest apologies."

"It's not your fault. Do what you can for now. I'll have a chat with my boss, see if we can post an officer outside the room. I'll be in touch soon." She didn't hang around for a response from the nurse. She jabbed the End Call button and shouted, "Shit, shit, shit."

"All right, you're going to need to calm down or you're not going to be able to think straight, Sam."

"But the perp was there. That's unforgiveable of me not to action something sooner." She thumped her thighs with her clenched fists.

Bob pulled over on double yellow lines, turned in his seat and grabbed one of her hands. "You need to stop that. I'm not going to sit here and listen to you spouting crap like that, you hear me?"

"I hear you, but I've let him down. Bugger, we should get to the hospital, check if this maniac has done anything to Rhys."

"Okay, I'll head over there now. In the meantime, you're going to have to speak to Armstrong, get him to agree to station an officer outside Rhys' room."

"Yes, you're right. Oh, Bob, what have I done?"

"Correction, you haven't done anything wrong. You weren't to know this idiot would strike again."

"True, however, I should have been prepared. The one day I decide to leave him… oh fuck, you don't suppose this warped individual has been watching me all the time I've been by Rhys' side, do you?"

Bob sighed. "I know this isn't what you want to hear, but yes, I think, without a doubt, that's a possibility."

"What are you waiting for, put your foot down, we need to get there ASAP."

Bob pressed the siren and grinned at her. "Your wish is my command."

"And you can shut that noise off for a start, if I'm about to give Armstrong a call."

"Oh shit, I forgot about that." He switched off the siren and waited for a gap to come his way in the traffic.

Sam gulped several times as she dialled DCI Armstrong's personal number. "Sorry to trouble you, sir, it's DI Cobbs here."

"Sam? What's going on? This isn't like you to reach out like this."

"I know, please forgive me, it's an urgent matter."

"Go on, I'm listening. How can I help?"

She explained the situation, relieved that her boss didn't try to interrupt her.

"Fuck! Excuse my language. Of course I'll sanction putting an officer outside his room. You should have gone ahead and actioned that sooner yourself."

"Thanks, sir. I didn't want to get accused of wasting funds."

"Don't be so ridiculous. Sounds like you're stressed. Do you want me to make the arrangements?"

"That would be brilliant, thanks, sir. I'm just on my way back to the hospital now, to check the perp hasn't done anything to Rhys that the nursing staff aren't aware of."

"Good idea. Leave this with me. Ring me after you leave the hospital, let me know what's going on."

"I will. I can't thank you enough for your support, it means a lot to me."

"Nonsense. He's a victim of an horrendous crime. We'd do the same for anyone else in his predicament, wouldn't we?"

"Absolutely. I'll be in touch soon." She ended the call, tipped back her head and released the breath she'd been holding in.

"Hey, see, you were worrying about nothing. I don't mean about the idiot visiting Rhys, I'm talking about whether Armstrong would back you or not. You're one of his best officers, Sam, he was hardly going to say no."

"I wish I was as confident about that as you are at times. He has his moments. I get the sense he tries his hardest to distance himself from those around him."

"I'll have to take your word for that, it's not like I know him as well as you do. Are you sure you don't want me to use the siren? It's getting busy up ahead."

Sam tutted. "It's your call."

"Yes!" Bob flicked the switch again and put his foot down. "This is more like it. It's an emergency call after all."

"Sadly true, although I wish it wasn't." *If only we weren't so far away from the hospital. Please be okay, Rhys. We'll get there as fast as we can, I promise you.*

"You've gone quiet on me again. That wouldn't have anything to do with my driving, would it?"

She laughed. "No, lost in thought, as usual. I feel safe with you driving, don't worry about that."

"Good. I've taken my advanced driving course and passed with flying colours."

"Yada, yada, as you've told me soooo many times before. It doesn't mean that I'm willing to give up my driving duties, matey. My car, my rules, end of."

"You can be such a… I'll leave you to fill in the blank."

Sam grinned. "'Wonderful partner' I think are the words you were searching for."

"Yeah, if you say so. We're not far away now. How are you feeling?"

"A bit calmer than I was talking to Armstrong. I hope he's stuck to his word and actioned our requirements."

"Hark at you, 'actioned our requirements'. You mean put an officer on duty at the hospital."

"That's what I said, didn't I?"

"Hardly. I'm sure, like me, he won't let you down."

"What would I do without you by my side, Bob?"

"Is this a trick question?"

She thumped him in the thigh.

"Ouch, what was that for?"

"Playing the village idiot when I'm trying to be nice. I won't bother in the future."

"Sorry, just teasing you. I was trying to get your mind off what lies ahead of us."

"I know, and I appreciate your thoughtfulness, even if it turns out to be a little clumsy at times."

"Get away with you, I've got no idea what you're talking about."

Sam glanced out of the side window at the fields as they whizzed past, but her stomach stirred too much and she ended up looking in front of her again. "How long before we get there? I don't recognise this part of the road."

"Around ten minutes. Don't worry, it's all in hand."

"Good, I'm relieved."

CHAPTER 5

Right on cue, they arrived at the hospital ten minutes later. "I'll drop you off at the front door and then search for a space, you know what a nightmare that can be around here."

"Thanks, Bob. There's usually a glut of them at the back, down the hill."

"That's bloody miles away," he complained. "Oh well, don't expect to see me too soon. How long shall I put on the meter?"

"Two hours. There's a bag of coins stashed in the little compartment just at the side of the steering wheel."

"Handy. Okay, I'll pay if I have enough cash on me."

"Whatever. I'm off." Sam sprinted out of the car and crashed through the main entrance. Then she wound her way through the older parts of the hospital that led her to Rhys' room. She let out a relieved breath when she saw the officer on guard. "Hi, I'm DI Sam Cobbs. Have you checked the room?"

"Yes, the nurse was in there when I arrived. She said there

didn't seem anything wrong with the patient. He was still asleep."

"Thanks. Are you aware of the situation?"

"Yes, the desk sergeant filled me in. Don't worry, ma'am, no one will get past me."

"I believe the perp was watching me. I've been here for hours on end; the moment I decide to go back to work, he strikes. No idea what his motive was for the attack or what his intentions are for coming to visit him so openly. Please remain vigilant at all times."

"You have my word. Umm… while you're here, would it be okay if I nipped to the loo? Sorry to ask, I didn't get the chance to go at the station before I left."

"Go, it's fine. I'll be here for a while yet; my partner is parking the car. Have you eaten? Now might be the best time for you to shove some food and a drink down your neck, while we're around."

"Gotcha. I'll grab a sandwich and a drink from the kiosk at reception. I won't be long."

The young officer marched along the corridor and passed Bob at the end.

"Down here, Bob. I'll see you inside." She pointed at the room she was about to enter, and he gave her a thumbs-up in response.

Sam eased herself into the seat beside Rhys. His breathing appeared to be back to normal. She waited for Bob to enter and then went in search of one of the nurses, to check how Rhys was really doing. "I won't be long. Take a seat, let me know if he stirs."

"Damn, he still looks very pale to me."

"He's not out of the woods yet, Bob."

She left the room and walked into the nearby ward to speak with the nurses. "Hi, I spoke to someone on the phone earlier regarding Rhys."

"Ah, yes, that was me. I'm so sorry about the mix-up, if that's what we can call it. We had no idea he didn't have any siblings. I admit, we're too trusting at times, but there would be uproar if we started asking people for their IDs before letting them in to visit a patient."

"I know, it's a tough call. Has someone examined Rhys since?"

"Yes, I checked all his vital signs; they were the same as they were a few hours ago. I really don't think the person who visited him did any harm."

"Let's hope you're right. Could they have had access to his drip?" Sam asked the most obvious question, and the nurse's cheeks coloured up.

"Yes. I changed the bag over as soon as I realised that was a possibility."

"Thank you, that's a load off my mind. Going forward, no one apart from staff is allowed to see him unless accompanied by me, is that clear?"

"Perfectly clear. And how long will the officer be on duty outside his room?"

"As long as he needs to be. There will be someone in attendance around the clock for the foreseeable, until Rhys is well enough to come home with me. Any idea how long that is likely to be?"

"Not yet. In all honesty, we expected him to be fully awake by now. When patients are asleep this long it's usually their body telling them they've not recovered enough to go home. So, patience will definitely need to be on the agenda for the next few days."

"Thanks. Are his parents still calling regularly?"

"Yes, they have been, up until now."

"That's good to hear. They're busy people, apparently."

The nurse smiled. "It's obvious to us how much you love him. Does it really matter if you're his only visitor?"

Sam shrugged. "I don't know, I feel his parents should make more of an effort, especially as his life was in danger the first few days."

The nurse smiled and nodded but said nothing further.

Sam returned to Rhys and Bob. She collected another chair from the corner of the room and sat opposite her partner. "Has he showed any signs of coming around?" Her gaze shifted to the drip, to make sure the nurse had told her the truth. There seemed to be a new bag in place.

"What's going on in that head of yours?"

"Nothing, just checking everything is okay. The nurse said they'd changed his drip after the stranger left."

"Wow, that must be a relief, to know they're so on the ball around here."

"Yeah, they do appear to be, which I'm grateful for. I wonder if they checked under the sheet."

"Want me to give you two some privacy?" He smirked.

"Don't be so ridiculous. What do you think I'm going to do, give him a handjob?"

Bob's eyes widened. "Umm… that thought never crossed my mind."

"Bollocks, as if." Sam tentatively lifted the sheet and peered underneath it. Rhys was still dressed in a hospital gown, his hairy legs bare.

"Anything under there, other than the obvious?" Bob asked.

"Nothing from what I can tell." And then she saw a slip of paper poking out from underneath Rhys' back. "What's this? Shit, have you got a pair of gloves on you?"

Bob shook his head and then saw a box of gloves on the bedside table on Sam's side. "There, beside you?"

"Any closer and they would have bitten me."

"What have you found?" Bob left his seat and came to assist her.

"I think there's a piece of paper underneath him." She snapped on a pair of gloves. "Can you hold the sheet up for me?"

"Consider it done. Wait, what are we going to put it in? Let me see if the nurses have got a plastic bag lying around."

"Good shout." Bob tore out of the room and seconds later returned with a Ziplock bag. "We're in luck."

They assumed their positions once more. Sam raised Rhys' gown to get a better view of what she suspected was a note and tugged at it gently.

"Is it coming? Sorry, wrong thing to say, given the circumstances."

Sam tutted. "Shut up, this is a delicate operation."

Bob laughed. "I'm sure it is. Christ, if anyone came in here now… well, I dread to think what they'd make of the situation."

"Ssh…" she reprimanded. A final tug, and the paper was free. She could tell it was indeed a note because, although it was folded, she could see some words written on the inside. "Here we go, let's see what this is all about."

They took a step back, and Sam held the note so they could both read it at the same time.

DI Cobbs, this is a warning to you and your team not to underestimate us. We gained access to Rhys' room easily enough, you'd be wise to consider that going forward.

This is just the beginning… you're going to need your wits about you for what we have planned for you.

Never judge a book by its cover, a lesson I was taught years ago by my father, someone who you knew very well.

Don't worry, our paths will cross sooner than you think.

TTFN.

. . .

"Wʜᴀᴛ ᴛʜᴇ ꜰᴜᴄᴋ? So what this person is effectively saying is, this is personal."

"Er… we kind of knew that, didn't we?" Bob asked, his confusion evident in the frown tugging at his brow.

"No, you don't understand. It's personal to *me*, not to Rhys. Shit, if he wasn't going out with me, he wouldn't be lying in a hospital bed right now."

"Ah, right. I'm with you. We're going to need to get that to the lab ASAP."

Sam read the note a second time, through tears of frustration that had welled up, and then tucked the piece of paper into the bag Bob was holding open for her.

"I can't believe this is happening," she said, stunned. She stared at the man she loved more than anyone else in this world, and the tears dripped onto her cheeks. Her shoulders shook as her resilience took a battering.

Bob flung an arm around her shoulder. "Hey, you can't do that. You're better than this, Sam. Don't give up at the first hurdle."

"But what if whoever is coming after me, doesn't hold back next time? If he's savvy enough to get in here this morning, or to put Rhys in hospital in the first place, who's to say what his next move is going to be?"

"Don't worry, we'll catch the bastard."

"CCTV footage, we need to get that sorted before we leave. It's our only hope of identifying the culprit."

"You're right. I'll get on it right away. We've got this, Sam. Stay positive."

She faced him and smiled. "I'm glad you're with me. Thanks, Bob."

"Do you want me to stay or go and sort out the footage?"

"The latter. I'll be okay. They say it's good to cry now and again, don't they?"

"Yeah, if you believe in all that crap. I won't be long, although I hate leaving you when you're feeling down like this."

"I'm not, not really. Go, that's an order."

He surprised her by pecking her on the cheek before he left the room. She held her hand to the spot where he'd kissed her.

You might be a royal pain in the arse at times, but underneath it all, you have a heart of gold, Bob Jones. I'm lucky to have you as my partner.

Sam sat next to Rhys and gently caressed his hand. It upset her that he didn't respond to her touch. It didn't take long for her attention to return to the note lying on the bedside table next to her.

Who could the perpetrator's father be? I've arrested and banged up so many criminals over the years, I really wouldn't know where to begin. If he's telling me this is just the beginning, what else has he got in store for me?

A light knock on the door disturbed her wayward thoughts. She left her seat and answered it rather than shout. "Hi, is that you back now?" she asked the uniformed officer.

"I am. I stopped at the kiosk and ate there. I hope that was okay, ma'am?"

"Of course it was. Sorry, what's your name?"

"It's Eddie Fox."

"Okay, Eddie, step inside a moment, I need to have a private word with you."

He followed her into the room, his brow creased. Sam collected the note and showed it to him.

"Bloody hell. Did you find that in this room, ma'am?"

"Correction, in his bed, under his body. It gives me a clear indication that we're dealing with someone who has balls and is not scared if he gets caught in the act. I showed you this to let you know what we're up against here. You're going to need to remain alert and vigilant at all times."

"You've got it, of course I will. Jesus, whoever left that note and did this to your fella, is a grade-one nutjob."

Sam smiled. "I couldn't have put it better myself, although I'm also tempted to call him a whole glut of bad names. What time do you knock off?"

"I'm due to finish at six."

"Okay, I'm presuming a colleague will be taking over from you."

He nodded.

"If you could emphasise to them the need to stop strangers coming into the room and to keep a watchful eye open in case anyone creeps up on them. The note clearly states that the attack on Rhys was just the beginning of what this tosser has in store for me and my team, and possibly Rhys."

"Don't worry, ma'am, I'll ensure I get the point across to whoever takes over from me. If there's anything else I can do to help, you only have to ask."

"I can't think of anything, not right now." A lightbulb went off in her mind. "Yes, I can. I'll have a word with the nursing staff, get the names of all those who are likely to be on duty over the next twenty-four hours, nurses and doctors. When I get back, I'll give you the list. You can then refuse access to anyone else who tries to enter the room, just in case the perp decides to nick a uniform with the intention of getting at Rhys again. I know that probably sounds like cloak-and-dagger stuff, something you're more likely to come across on the TV, but I'd rather put it in place all the same."

"It makes sense to me, ma'am."

Sam nodded and headed towards the nurses' station. She

made the nurse on duty aware of what had happened in her absence and the need for them to be extra cautious going forward. The nurse agreed with Sam's plan and told her to give her ten minutes to pull all the names together.

"That'd be great. I'll collect it in a little while."

"It's okay. I'll bring it to you. Do you want to use one of our clipboards as well?"

"You're amazing. Thanks so much for all your help."

"It's the least we can do after what's happened."

"You're too kind."

Sam returned to Rhys' room to find him stirring. "Hey, you. How are you?"

He turned his head towards her, and a glimmer of a smile emerged. He whispered something, but she didn't quite catch what he said. She placed her head closer to his lips, and he tried again.

"Hello, my angel. I've missed you."

Tears pricked her eyes, and she had trouble holding them back. She kissed him on the lips and gently hugged him, relieved to have him conscious again. He coughed, so she took a step back, giving him room to breathe.

"I'm sorry, I shouldn't have crowded you. How are you feeling now?"

"All the better for seeing you. What's going on with me? Why am I still in hospital?"

"You had some internal bleeding they needed to sort out. You haven't been well enough to come home, love. You need to get some of your strength back before they discharge you. I'm going to call the nurse, let her know you're awake."

He raised his hand, and she gripped it with both of hers.

"No, I just want to be alone with you for a little while, if that's all right?"

"Only for a few minutes then, the nurse should check you over. Are you in any pain?"

"Yes, I have a throbbing sensation in my groin every time I look at you, and my heart beats rapidly when I think about what I'm going to do to you when I get you home."

Sam laughed. "You flirt. You're too funny. Hey, it's going to be a while before you're able to exert yourself."

He wiggled his eyebrows and whispered, "There are ways around that."

The door opened, and Bob entered the room. "Oops, sorry, am I interrupting?"

Sam rested her head against Rhys' and whispered, "Don't you dare tell him what's going on in that mind of yours." She stood again, her eyes wide, warning him what would happen to him if he went against her wishes.

"No, come in, Bob. It's good to see you," Rhys said.

Bob approached the other side of the bed. "Hey, not as good as it is to see you. Glad you're awake and on the road to recovery."

Sam smiled. "Can you give us a minute, Rhys? I won't be long." She motioned for Bob to join her outside the room. "I didn't want you putting your foot in it about obtaining the footage."

"As if I would? Grant me some sense. He seems pretty bright in there. How long has he been awake?"

"He's only just come around. How did you get on?"

"The security guard was shit-hot, he found the footage straight away."

"Of the perpetrator? He was caught on camera?"

"Yes and no."

"Don't tell me, he was dressed all in black and wearing a hoodie?"

"A plus for hitting the nail on the head. We observed the guy on the camera, and he appeared to walk towards a blue van at the rear of the car park, but the camera failed to pick up whether or not he got in the vehicle. We tried different cameras and saw the van leaving around the same time."

"Could you read the reg?" Sam asked hesitantly, already sensing what his answer was going to be.

"There wasn't one on the back, and we couldn't find any images of the van from the front. The guard is going to search the other discs, check if he can see when the van arrived. He's going to get back to me later."

"Okay, I suppose that will have to do for now. Did you take a photo of this bastard?"

Bob grinned. "I knew you'd ask me. As it happens, I did." He withdrew his phone and showed Sam the image he'd snapped.

"Bugger, it's not much, but hopefully it'll be enough to bring this fucker down when we finally arrest him and the case goes to court." She showed the photo to Eddie. "Want us to send you a copy?"

"No, it's fine, ma'am. I'll keep an eye out for him."

"Right, Bob, why don't you get yourself a coffee? I just want to spend ten minutes with Rhys before we head off."

"Absolutely. Go for it. Do you want me to bring you one back?"

"I'm fine, thanks all the same."

The nurse appeared and gave Sam the list she'd cobbled together.

"Thanks, this is great." She handed it to Eddie and returned to the room to find Rhys with his eyes closed. She crept on tiptoe towards the bed and gently kissed his forehead. "Are you awake?"

"I am. Do you have to go now? I take it you're back at work."

"Yes, I went back this morning, and no, I can stay with you for another ten minutes and then I have to fly." She sat next to him and clasped his hand which felt warm and sticky.

"Are you hot? Do you need anything? Damn, I forgot to tell the nurse you're awake."

"Don't, not yet. I just want to spend some time with my favourite person."

"Well, that's nice to hear. Can I ask you about the incident? Are you up to talking about it?"

"We can try."

"Can you go over what happened?"

"I think I was on my way back from the baker's. I was close to my building when this young guy came out of nowhere and blocked my path. I asked him politely to let me pass, but every time I took a step sideways, he jumped in my way again, preventing me from getting past him. I felt intimidated so, while I was talking to him, I took a few steps back. He came towards me, started shouting all sorts, and then withdrew a knife. I think I dropped my lunch and tried to talk him around."

"Can you tell me what he was saying?"

"He told me that the likes of me were a drain on society."

"He what? What a bizarre thing to say. Did you recognise him?"

"No, he was young, late teens, but I don't recall ever seeing him before. Saying that, my attention was drawn to the knife most of the time. I pleaded with him to put the weapon down and to speak with me. He told me he was done talking with cranks like me and there was only going to be one end to what was about to happen."

"He said that, word for word?"

"Near as I can remember, yes. He seemed to be a confused young man. Maybe he saw the plaque outside my office, stating my title, and it had a devastating effect on him mentally."

"Do you think he's had a bad experience with a psychiatrist in the past?"

"Maybe. That's how it was coming across to me."

"Was it just him? Did anyone else show up after he stabbed you?"

"I don't think so. I was intent on calling for the ambulance and contacting you. Did I do the right thing, Sam?"

"Of course you did. Calling the ambulance probably saved your life, love. You were in a terrible state when Bob and I got there. The paramedics showed up not long after, and they were brilliant with you."

He inhaled a large breath. "I'm so glad I made it. I thought I was a goner and I was never going to lay eyes on you again."

She leaned over and kissed him. "You're going to be fine, I'm not going anywhere, hon, except back to the station, soon. I'll call in later, on my way home. Do you need anything?"

"Only you."

She was floored by the love evident in his eyes. It almost knocked her sideways, and she wasn't sure how to react. "That's a given. You've got me, whether you want me or not, matey."

"Good to know. I'm sorry, I'm getting tired again now."

"I'll let the nurses know that you woke up but you've gone back to sleep again. I'll see you after work. I love you, Rhys."

"Right backatcha," he mumbled before his eyes flickered shut.

Sam crept out of the room, made the nurses aware that she'd had a reasonable conversation with him and that he'd gone back to sleep. The nurse thanked her and told her she would check on Rhys the next time she was passing.

"I'll be back later, probably at around six."

"See you then."

Sam ensured Eddie knew what to do in her absence and then made her way downstairs to find Bob. He was sitting in the coffee shop with tell-tale crumbs on his chin.

"Enjoy your chocolate muffin, did you?" She picked up his napkin and encouraged him to wipe his face.

"It would have been rude of me not to partake in some of the goodies on offer. Want me to get you one?"

"No. I'd rather get to the lab ASAP."

He shot out of his chair. "Damn, I forgot all about that."

She raised an eyebrow. "Luckily for you, I hadn't. I don't suppose you stopped by the security guard's office again?"

"I didn't, he said he was going to text me later."

"Okay, let's get out of here."

SAM DECIDED to see if Des was in his office after she dropped the note off to the lab techs. He wasn't, he was performing the PM on Gabby Addis. She knocked on the door to his theatre to gain his attention. Des glanced up and gestured for her to join him.

She opened the door. "We can't, we're not suited and booted. I wondered how things were going."

"I've found traces of skin under her fingernails."

"What are you saying? You think she was murdered?"

"Yes. Before I turned her over, I discovered slight bruising on her back and on her ankles. There are also scratches on the front of her thighs, as though she was placed on the edge of the window before being thrown out."

"Okay, that makes sense. I had an inkling that was going to be the result. She wasn't the type to commit suicide. According to her father, she had too much going for her."

Des nodded and asked, "Any news on her son?"

"Nothing as yet. Maybe he's the reason she was killed, to gain access to the child. Gotta fly, we have a few leads we need to chase up."

"What are you doing here if you didn't come to see me?"

"Rhys had a visit from the person who attacked him. They

left a note, addressed to me. I've dropped it off at the lab, hoping they'll find some prints on it."

"It was personal then, is that what you're saying?"

"Looks that way. I'll catch up with you later."

"I hope the attack on Rhys doesn't distract you from dealing with this case."

Sam stared at him in disbelief. "You really don't know me very well at all, do you?"

He flinched as if she'd slapped him around the face. "Sorry, I shouldn't have said that out loud."

"Ah, but you did, Des. I'm going before this conversation gets too heated." She closed the door and thought she heard him shout an apology, but she wasn't sure.

"Are you all right?" Bob caught up with her as she marched back up the hallway towards the car park.

"I need some fresh air."

"I don't think he meant anything by his comment. He's got a tendency to speak before he engages his brain."

"Must be a man thing, right? Because you have the same problem periodically, too."

"I… er… yep, it would be foolish of me to deny it."

BACK AT THE STATION, Sam gathered the team around and then went over what Gabby's father had told them. "So, we've got several leads to investigate. A former boyfriend, Vince Hardy; the father didn't know if he was still in the area or not. We've yet to visit her place of work, see what her staff have to say, so that should be our next stop, Bob. Also, we need to keep on top of the search for the boy. Plus, when we spoke to the pathologist earlier, he told me his preliminary assessment is that Gabby was most likely murdered."

"What about the ex-boyfriend?" Claire asked. "Is he the father of the child?"

Sam went over her notes. "No, his father was Marlon Bobbin who died three years ago."

"Would it be worth considering his family? See if anything shows up in their backgrounds?" Claire added.

"Always worth a shot. Although, when I asked her father if the family were still in contact with Gabby, he said yes, the boy stayed with his grandparents a few times a month."

"Maybe we should consider visiting the grandparents, just in case the boy shows up there," Oliver suggested.

"Bob and I are going to be up to our necks in it this afternoon. Do you want to take that task on, Oliver?"

"I'd love to, boss. Shall I take someone with me?"

"Yes, Alex, can you tag along for the ride?"

"If I have to." He grinned.

"Right, I need the rest of you to carry out the necessary searches, i.e. Gabby's social media and bank accounts, see what shows up there. Are you ready for the off again, Bob?"

He rose from his seat. "I'm up and down like a whore's knickers today."

Sam rolled her eyes. "A distasteful and unwarranted analogy, partner."

"Oops, sorry."

"No, you're not."

"You're right, I'm not."

They drew up outside Addis Recruitment which was situated in the middle of Workington. Sam was surprised to find a parking space at that time of the day. "Are you ready for this?"

"Yep, let's do it."

They entered via the front doorway, and Sam did a quick head count before the receptionist had the chance to say hello. *Blimey, ten staff, unless there are more of them out the back.*

She and Bob flashed their warrant cards at the brunette who appeared to be over-friendly with Bob.

"Oh, the police, that's a novelty. What can I do for you?" She fluttered her eyelashes at Bob half a dozen times.

Sam found the display highly amusing, despite the grim circumstances that had brought them to the agency. Bob fidgeted beside her.

She finally put him out of his misery by speaking up. "Is the manager around? Or person in charge here today?"

"Ah, the owner is absent, but her second-in-command, Zach Elliott, is here. Would you like a word?" the receptionist replied stiffly.

"Thanks, that would be great."

"I'll see if Mr Elliott is available. Do you want to take a seat?"

"We're okay standing," Sam responded curtly, proving the woman was no match for her.

The young woman tottered off to the right and went through an archway that presumably led to the manager's office. She returned a few moments later wearing a smug grin that Sam was tempted to swipe off her face. "I'm sorry, Zach's rather busy at present. Can you call back in a couple of hours?"

"Sorry, that's not convenient for us. If he's too busy to see us, can you ask him if he'll allow us to speak with the other members of staff, please?"

"Umm… I can ask. What's this about?"

"I think the manager should be given that information before anyone else, don't you?"

The woman huffed and mumbled something as she swished her hair over her shoulder, Sam sensed it was for Bob's benefit, and then walked back through the archway. Her visit with Zach took longer this time and resulted in him returning with her.

"Is there a problem here?" he asked, seemingly perplexed as he appraised them both.

"Is there somewhere private we can speak, sir?"

"In my office, but I'm in the middle of dealing with some very important clients. I only left them because Miranda said you were being difficult with her."

"We were? That's news to me," Sam said. Her gaze shifted to the beautiful Miranda for clarification.

"I… ummm… well, I asked them if they wouldn't mind coming back in a couple of hours like you suggested, but they refused. If that's not being difficult, I'm not sure what is."

"I agree with her. We have an important business to oversee here, and we can't just drop everything the second two police officers descend upon us, demanding to be seen. As it is, I'm filling in for the owner of the company, who was due to see the client today. Unfortunately, neither of us has been able to contact Gabby during the day. It would be rude of me to tell the clients that I can no longer see them at such short notice, don't you agree, Inspector?"

"Ordinarily, yes, I would wholeheartedly agree with you, however, we wouldn't be here if our need wasn't urgent, I can assure you."

"Urgent? Would you care to explain?"

By now, the rest of the staff had stopped what they were doing and were listening to their conversation. "I'm sorry, as I've already told you, it's a private matter, one that I would rather discuss with you in person, Mr Elliott."

His hand spread across his chest, he asked, "Me, as in personally? As in I have done something wrong in the eyes of the law?"

Sam shook her head and sighed. *Give me strength!* "All will be revealed as soon as we can speak with you, without the need of an audience, sir."

She could see the hesitation in his eyes.

"Okay, Miranda, can you ask the clients if they'd like a drink? Tell them that an unforeseen emergency has come up that needs my immediate attention and that I'll be with them in five minutes."

Miranda lowered her voice, so the rest of the staff couldn't hear. "I don't have to point out how unprofessional that is going to make the agency look, do I, Zach?"

"You're right, you don't have to point out the obvious; in fact, I wish you wouldn't. Come through." He opened the flap in the counter so that Sam and Bob followed him, past the gobsmacked receptionist, into an office through the archway. "We'll go into my office as the clients are in Gabby's." He opened the door but remained just inside the room, giving Sam and Bob the space to squeeze in behind him. Folding his arms, he said, "Please make it quick. As Miranda just said, we're a professional company who have high standards to meet."

"As you wish. You stated before that Gabby Addis hadn't been seen at the office all day. Perhaps you can tell me when you last saw her?"

"What sort of question is that?"

"An essential one. So, if you wouldn't mind answering it."

"We left here at around six last night. Gabby had already gone home; she had to pick Tyler up from the school at about three and then continued to work from home, in her office. We held a Zoom meeting at around eight last night, once she'd put Tyler to bed."

"And what was the meeting about, can you tell me?"

"Yes, about the clients I'm dealing with at the moment. Gabby wanted everything to go smoothly because there's a possibility that they can bring in tens of thousands of new business in the near future, another reason why I should be in there now, speaking with them."

"Okay, I think you need to take a seat before we go any further."

"I'm all right standing, thanks all the same. I sense the time is ticking for us all, Inspector. Tell me what this is all about. Wait... why are you asking about Gabby? Has something happened to her?" His eyes held a terror as the penny dropped.

"Yes, unfortunately, Gabby's body was found at her property this morning, by her cleaner."

"What? No! I can't believe this... not Gabby. She can't be dead, how? How did this happen?"

"The reason we're here today is because we believe Gabby was murdered, but the murderer set the scene up to make it look like she had killed herself."

He spun around and ran both his hands through his hair and then placed them on the top of his head. "Jesus... this can't be true. Gabby was only young, she had everything to live for. Gave her career her all. Won awards because of her determination. There's no way she would ever kill herself. Jesus, what about Tyler?"

"Regrettably, he was missing from the property when the cleaner arrived. There's an alert out for him; every on-duty officer is searching the streets. Up until now, there have been no sightings of the child."

"Fuck, fuck, fuck! Sorry, I shouldn't be swearing, but this news has been like a bolt of lightning striking me. She was in good spirits last night. Tyler was in her office with her, playing happily with his toys."

"She didn't seem anxious or stressed in the slightest?"

"No, but then Gabby had mastered how to deal with her stress, she'd had to, fairly quickly, once the client list started growing and the awards for excellence began rolling in." He fell silent and paced the room. As he passed a chair, he kicked out at it, venting his anger. "Jesus, this is a nightmare, and I'm not sure how this will affect the morale of the team. I'm sorry, that seems a selfish thing to say... you have to understand, she was a boss in a million. She treated everyone as if they were her dear friends. She was a special lady, a very special boss, who cared about what the staff thought. Making us an excellent team. The others will back me up, tell you the same."

"I'm sure. As you were close to her, had she mentioned lately anything that might have been concerning her?"

"Concerning her? In what respect?"

"Either with the business or in her personal life? Was she seeing anyone?"

"No, it was just her and Tyler at home. She told me she was determined not to be one of those women who brought a flurry of men through their front door, giving her son a reason to question her behaviour. She was devoted to him, always putting his needs before hers."

"And the business was going well?"

"Actually, better than that, it was exceptional. Since she won—we won, as a team—a prestigious award for business of the year, our client base has doubled."

"And the staff have been able to deal with the increase?"

"Yes, she had the foresight to know that the workload was about to explode and set out to employ extra staff to cope with the demand. It took her six months to find the right people to join us; she was very particular with how this agency should be run. Putting the clients' needs above everything else." He paused to take a breath and shook his head, then he moved towards the desk and perched his backside on the edge. "I still can't get my head around this. The thought of us never sharing a cup of coffee over a client's case or..." He glanced up and stared at Sam. "I'm lost for what to say next. My mind is clouding over with bad thoughts. Are you sure she's been murdered?"

"We're going off the preliminary findings of the post-mortem, but yes, there are certain elements to the way she was found that have puzzled us. I can't really say more about that at this moment."

"Why? God almighty, this can't be real. And where the heck is Tyler? Those two were inseparable, loved the bones of each other. Her whole life revolved around Tyler's needs and running this business. She picked her staff carefully, to ensure those around her had the same vision she had, allowing her to spend more time at home with her son. Hang on, you're not telling me that whoever… killed Gabby has taken Tyler, are you?"

Sam shrugged. "We can't answer that question. All we know is what the cleaner told us: Tyler wasn't at the property when she arrived there this morning."

"Christ, I'm struggling to comprehend how massive this is. Not only have I lost one of the best colleagues—no, bosses—I've ever had the fortune to work with, but her child, the son she adored, has gone missing as well."

"Which is why we felt the need to interrupt your meeting today. At the moment, we don't have many leads to go on. I was wondering if you could change that."

"Me? How?"

"By telling us if Gabby had received any threats or unwanted attention from anyone lately."

He frowned and contemplated her question. "No, I can't think of anything. Gabby and I were really close. I'm sure she would have told me if she'd been worried about anything."

"I have to ask, if this business is classed as being super successful, has there been any problems with your competitors in the past?"

"I can't recall anything. It's not the type of business that could be classed as competitive or stepping on other companies' toes, not like in the fashion industry or a career along those lines."

"Thanks, I hadn't really considered that. How many recruitment agencies of this calibre are there in the area?"

"We're the only ones who are worth speaking to, but then, I would say that, wouldn't I? No, honestly, we're a top-class company, and there isn't another of our standing in Cumbria, let alone the west coast of the region. That's why we won the award for the whole of northern England. That type of accolade isn't dished out willy-nilly, you know."

"And who decides who wins the awards?"

"The industry decides."

"Just to clarify, are you telling me that your competitors have a vote or does a governing body oversee the awards and who is eligible to receive them?"

"The latter. That's what makes it fair, in my opinion."

Sam nodded her agreement. "What about after work, when it's time to shut up the office for the day? Have you noticed anyone lurking around the car park or spotted someone acting suspiciously at the end of the day?"

"No, I don't recall anything at all along those lines. I'd be the first to jump in there and sort them out if there was any kind of shenanigans going on. We have a lot of female colleagues who work here; most of the men are protective of them. You hear so many horror stories happening to the fairer sex these days… sorry, of course, you'd know all about the statistics, being a police officer. I didn't mean anything derogatory by that comment."

"I agree, crimes against women are on the increase throughout the UK, something that we have to combat every day, but you're telling me you haven't seen any sign of any strangers at all keeping an eye on the place."

"If they have, then I haven't seen them. Couldn't this be a random attack on Gabby? I've always had my doubts whether living in such an isolated house was the right thing for her and Tyler."

"You told her that?"

"Yes, on several occasions. She told me I was being silly and that she had always felt safe in her surroundings. Loved her house and the solitude of the area. Tyler loved it there, too. There was talk about them getting a puppy for him when he got older. It's not as if they didn't have a large enough garden for it... sorry, I'm waffling."

"You're allowed. This type of news sometimes makes people react uncharacteristically. Is there anything else you can tell us that might give us a lead as to who did this to Gabby?"

"I'm sorry, I wish I could think of something. I can't."

"Don't worry. We don't want to hold you up any longer than is necessary. Here's my card. If anything comes to mind after we've left, feel free to call me."

"Thanks for understanding my need to get back to the clients. I just hope I can hold it together during our meeting and that I do Gabby proud. I'll show you out."

"I'm sure you'll be able to pull it off. Would it be possible if we had a quick chat with the rest of the staff?"

"Oh yes, I don't see why not. Would you rather I break the news to them first?"

"It might be for the best."

Rather than shout, he drew his colleagues' attention with a quick clap of his hands and asked them to come and join them. "I'm going to make this quick, only because I have clients waiting for me... oh God, I thought I'd be able to do this but I'm struggling to find the right words." He peered over his shoulder at Sam. "Can you help me out here?"

Sam patted him on the back. "Why don't you get back to your clients and I'll fill your staff in with the news?"

"Sounds good to me. Sorry, folks. Listen carefully to what

the officer has to say, and we'll discuss what we need to do going forward, after I've finished my meeting." Then he took off, faster than a hare out of the traps.

Sam prepared herself by inhaling a couple of deep breaths as she surveyed the puzzled faces of the men and women in front of her. "It is with regret that I have to inform you that your boss, Gabby Addis, was found dead at her home first thing this morning."

Every member of the team either gasped or swore under their breath. Sam scrutinised each and every one of them in turn, hoping to spot something which would give her an indication that one of them knew something about Gabby's death, but she didn't pick up on anything untoward going on with any of them.

"All right, let's settle down, the last thing we want to do is disturb Zach."

"Do you know what happened to her?" Miranda asked.

"We can't really say at this time. What we wanted to ask all of you is whether Gabby has mentioned being worried or frightened about an issue going on in either her personal or working life."

"You're telling us, in not so many words, that she was killed? This wasn't an accident or that she died from natural causes?" the tallest member of the team, a male, said at the back.

"That's correct. But again, that's the only detail I'm willing to divulge at present, in case it hampers our investigation. Can any of you help us out? I would normally interview you all separately, one by one, but I'm desperate to get on with the case."

"Jesus, this is unbelievable," one of the older women said. "Oh, no, I've just had a thought, what about little Tyler? He isn't dead as well, is he?"

"No, at least, we don't think so. His body wasn't found at

the property. As far as we know he's gone missing. We're not sure what that means, he might have run off or the killer abducted him. That's as much as I can tell you regarding her son."

Again, the group of men and women either gasped or swore.

"That poor boy," Miranda said. "He's been here a few times, he's such a sweetheart."

"I want to assure you, we're doing our utmost to find him. Has anyone got any idea who would want to either harm Tyler or kill his mother? Have you perhaps overheard something you shouldn't have around the office or outside the premises? Did Gabby ever confide in one of you that she was perhaps scared or if she had a bad feeling about someone she knew or had just met?" Sam had an idea she was going to leave the premises empty-handed, judging by the expressions of the people in front of her. "Nothing at all?" she prompted after being greeted by silence.

"Do her parents know?" a woman at the front asked.

"Yes, they're aware, they were informed a few hours ago."

The group fell silent, so Sam decided to hand out a bunch of her cards to them. "If you do think of anything after we've left, please, please give me a call ASAP. We're going to have to go now. Thank you for listening, and sorry to be the bearer of such sad news today."

Miranda took her card and muttered an apology for her earlier behaviour. "I'm sorry for the way I acted before. Had I known you were going to deliver such bad news…"

Sam smiled. "It's forgotten about." She motioned for Miranda to step to one side and said, "Can you keep your eyes and ears open for the next few days? I'm not saying this has anything to do with your colleagues but, in our experience, the culprits are generally known to the victim."

"Of course I will, but there's no way anyone around here

would have done this. We all admire and love, or should I say loved, Gabby so much. What you're seeing here is all of us in utter shock, even the men, and that rarely happens, I assure you. Do you have any leads at all?"

Sam shrugged. "Nothing as yet. Our priority remains with trying to find Tyler, to see what he can tell us about his mother's death. Other than that, we're going to be relying on the pathologist and his team to find clues and the evidence we need to move the investigation forward."

"I'll keep vigilant, it's the least I can do. Gabby was a wonderful, vibrant woman. I admired her so much. She set out as a teenager to be the best and accomplished that all by herself."

"Along with all of you, surely?"

"Not really. Everything was in place long before she opened this agency." Miranda tapped at her temple. "It was all up here with her; she was a thinker as well as a doer. By that I mean, her mind was constantly working up a storm, even when she was at home. There would be days when she arrived at work with a pad full of ideas for the next big thing. Some of which she discarded by the end of the week, but she was a lateral thinker who always had new ideas forming in her mind ready to replace those she had ditched. Truthfully, I've never known a woman like her. Not quite true, I worked for a lady a few years ago who had everything on her shoulders, but it put a lot of pressure on her marriage. She and her husband eventually split up, and he ended up with the two kids because she couldn't afford the time to care for them; he could, even though he was working full-time."

"Sorry to hear that, but Gabby managed to achieve all that she had, with a toddler to cope with as well. She sounds a remarkable individual."

Miranda teared up and plucked a tissue from the box sitting on the reception desk. "She was, we're all going to miss her. Do you need a hand, searching for Tyler? I know there are a few people around here who would be willing to drop what they're doing and help, if you need extra bodies out there to find the little mite."

"I'll bear it in mind. At the moment we have every available officer searching for him."

"I hope you find him, I truly do." She shuddered. "It makes my skin crawl to think of him in… well, a killer's hands."

"Try not to think about that. Leave that side of things for us to worry about. Thanks for your time. We're going to shoot off now, we have other people we need to interview before the day is out."

"Good luck. We'll put our thinking caps on after you leave. Hopefully, we'll come up with something useful for you."

"No matter how insignificant you believe an issue is, there's every chance it might turn out to be integral to solving the investigation."

"I promise, we'll do our best. We want this person caught as much as you do. She meant everything to us."

Sam nodded. "Thanks for your help. Hope to speak to you soon, should anything come to light."

Sam and Bob left the premises and walked back to the car.

"That was tough for them, and you," Bob said.

Sam unlocked the car and jumped in. "It was. Let's hope something comes from it. I'm going to contact Oliver before we set off."

She dialled the young officer's number, but his colleague, Alex, answered it. "Everything all right with all of you?"

"Yes, Oliver was making the grandmother a cup of tea. She's beside herself, as you can imagine."

"I bet. When was the last time she saw Gabby and Tyler?"

"A couple of weeks ago, they invited her to stay with them

for the weekend. She told us Gabby had a spot of work to do so she volunteered to take Tyler shopping while his mother worked. Gabby met up with them in Workington, and they went bowling together."

"Nothing untoward happened while she was with them?"

"Not that she can think of. She's really distraught; it might be worth checking back with her in a day or two."

"Okay, so it's unlikely she's behind the child's disappearance, is that what you're telling me?"

"One hundred percent. I'd bet my life on it, if it came down to it, boss."

"No need to go that far, Alex, I get your drift. All right, finish up there and meet us back at the station. Don't forget to show the woman some compassion, and don't leave until she seems better and able to cope."

"Don't worry, we wouldn't be that insensitive, boss."

"I apologise, I didn't mean to insinuate you would. As you were, see you back at base." She ended the call and slapped her thigh. "Damn, I really struggle giving that man a chance some days. And before you start on me, I've already admitted I was in the wrong."

"He's a good bloke. Maybe if you used him more out in the field, rather than choosing Oliver and Liam all the time, he wouldn't feel like his nose is being put out of joint most days."

Sam's mouth dropped open and she turned to face him. After a second or two, she composed herself enough to say, "What? Has he said something along those lines to you?"

"Not in so many words. He does feel like he's overlooked occasionally, though. I'm not criticising you, far from it, just letting you know where the land lies with him, that's all."

"What are you saying? That he's considering leaving us?"

"I wouldn't go that far. Is there a reason why you don't gel with him as much as the rest of the team?"

"Blimey, I hadn't realised things were that bad."

"They're not, however, the others have noticed your attitude is different towards him."

"Seriously? I… shit. I'm sorry, our conversation has totally shocked me."

"Hey, it's not that bad, not really."

"But noticeable all the same. I think I need to have a quiet word with Alex when we get back."

"To apologise?"

"Er… I wasn't considering that, more like sorting out any issues we might have with each other. Christ, now you've got me trawling through my mind, going over recent conversations I've had with him."

"And? What's your assessment of them? Go on, I'm intrigued to know."

"Umm… I'm not sure. Maybe there's a certain amount of truth in your words."

"In other words, you think I'm right, right?"

Sam started the engine and grinned at him. "Easy, tiger, I don't think those words ever entered my mind, let alone anywhere near the tip of my tongue, ready to escape."

"That figures."

She laughed. "What's that supposed to mean?"

"I think we'd better end this conversation before one of us ends up saying something they're likely to regret."

"Are you for real? How has this conversation taken this turn?"

"The ball has been in your court, you've been tossing it back and forth for a few minutes, I just played along with you."

"Shut up!"

"Whatever!"

CHAPTER 6

Casey ran around her house, picking up Hudson's toys, as if she was a woman possessed. Every day she ensured the house was tidy, knowing that if she let her standards slip it would take her forever to put things right, and she couldn't allow that to happen. She ran a successful gym in Workington and was in the process of raising the finances from the bank to open a new one in Whitehaven to try and do her bit for a town in desperate need of regeneration. Every time she'd been there lately, she discovered three more shops had closed down. She found it hard to believe that what had once been considered a thriving community, could now be on the verge of a retail apocalypse. Just like one of those apocalyptic-type movies she'd seen a few years back. Maybe the filmmakers had received some kind of premonition about what the future would hold for them.

The doorbell rang, drawing her out of her gloomy thought process. "Hudson, put that truck back in the box, you can play with it later, when we get back from the hospital." She was still shouting at her son when she opened the front door to find two workmen standing on her doorstep.

"Hi, can I help?" she asked warily, suddenly pulling the door to behind her.

"Morning, Mrs Pardoe. We're repairing what appears to be a blockage in the water mains outside the property, and it's come to our attention that the problem might lie here, caused by the feed from this property. Would it be all right if we had a quick gander? It shouldn't take us long."

Casey glanced at her watch. "You'd better make it quick, I'm due at the hospital in about an hour and I've got a five-year-old to get ready for the appointment."

"Oh, right, nothing serious, I hope?" the older man asked.

"No, just a checkup. It's a bloody nuisance if you must know, having to take Hudson out of school for the day and me having to have time off work." There's no way she was about to reveal what was really going on with her, not to a couple of strangers, she wasn't the type.

"A real inconvenience for you. We'll try and keep out of your way. There's a possibility the problem might lie within the house rather than outside the property. Would it be okay if we checked inside first, you know, what with you needing to go out?"

"Oh, yes, that makes perfect sense." Her gaze dropped to their footwear. "I hate to ask, but would you mind taking your shoes off? I've just had new carpet laid throughout the downstairs."

"Consider it done. Get them off, lad," the older man ordered.

The men removed their shoes, and she showed them through the house to the kitchen and the large utility room at the rear. "Mind if I leave you to it, what with me being on a tight schedule?"

"Go for it. We shouldn't keep you too long."

"Glad to hear it. Excuse me, won't you?" Casey continued with her cleaning spree in the front room, conscious of the time getting away from her. She still had the bathroom to clean and the washing to put out.

Damn, I should have warned the men I had some washing on. Still, they wouldn't have to be Einstein to figure that one out for themselves once the spin cycle kicks in.

"Hudson, Hudson, where are you?"

Her son often played hide and seek with her, once her full attention lay elsewhere. "I'm counting and will come and find you when I reach ten. One, two... tickle my shoe, three... four, the monster's at the door... I hope you're hiding somewhere good this time... five, six, a good handful of pick and mix... seven, eight, you better deliver an empty plate, later at teatime... nine, ten... I'm coming for you again. Here I come, ready or not." She searched his favourite place to hide, behind the couch, and then moved on to peek behind the two large easy chairs, but she had a feeling he wouldn't be there because he usually had to move them to squeeze through the gap. As far as she could tell, the furniture hadn't been moved. Failing to find her son in the lounge, she moved into the hallway, her gaze drifting up to the clock on the wall. Her heart racing, she climbed the stairs. "Are you up here, you cheeky little monkey? Hey, I'd better find you soon otherwise we're going to miss our appointment."

One of the workmen dropped one of his tools in the kitchen, startling her. For a moment, she had forgotten they were there. She ran along the hallway, briefly checking each of the rooms from the doorway until she reached Hudson's bedroom. She got down on her knees to look under the bed. It was clear, except for a few boxes of toys she'd shoved under there the week before.

"Where are you?" she muttered, knowing the time was fast getting away from them.

She left his room and nipped next door to her own. He wasn't in there either, or in the en suite. She ran back to the main bathroom and pulled back the shower curtain which was another of his favourite hiding places. Again, nothing there. She returned to the hallway and bellowed, "Okay, Hudson, I give in, you win. Where are you, love? Time is running out on us, and we have to get ready now."

She stood still, listening for any sign of movement. There was none. With only one more room to search, she rushed along the hallway to the box room at the end. There were plenty of nooks and crannies where Hudson could squeeze into but, again, he was nowhere to be seen.

"This isn't funny any more, sweetheart. Come on, you've won. We'll have an ice cream after we leave the hospital, that's a promise. Now show yourself."

"Hello, is this who you're looking for?" A voice sounded behind her at the top of the stairs.

She spun around so fast, she lost her balance and had to steady herself against the wall. "What... what are you doing with my son?" The way the man had his arm wrapped around her son's neck sent alarm bells ringing.

"I found him for you, I thought you'd be pleased," he said, his grin broadening.

Her stomach did several somersaults. She was already worked up about the time being against them, now she had to contend with this man holding her son hostage, at least that's what it looked like at first glance. Maybe she was doing him an injustice.

Casey called her son to her. "Come on, Hudson, let's get you ready for our little outing. Thanks for bringing him upstairs, where was he?" She tried to sound natural, all the time suppressing the fear mounting within.

"He came wandering into the kitchen. He rudely asked us what we were doing in his house."

"That was naughty, Hudson. The nice man is trying to look for a fault in the plumbing. Come to me, darling." She held out her hand, willing her son to come towards her, but when the man's arm tightened around his neck, she almost lost the contents of her stomach. "Can you let him go, please?"

"In good time. Now, let's see what games we can play of our own, shall we? Adam, can you bring the bag of goodies upstairs? I think we'll play up here today."

"What are you talking about?"

He laughed. "You'll see soon enough."

Casey sensed the man's mood had turned sinister. She inched forward, hopeful that he wouldn't have noticed.

"Stay where you are. We're coming to you, aren't we, Hudson? You want to be with Mummy, don't you, son?"

Casey fixed a smile in place in an effort not to scare her son any more than was necessary. She could see the terror in his eyes, and the sight of his pale cheeks gripped her heart.

What the fuck am I going to do? How can I get my son away from him? What the hell are they intending to do to me, to us? Shit, why did I let them in?

"I can see the cogs turning," the man said in a singsong voice that annoyed the hell out of her.

"What do you want from me?"

"Hmm… let me think about that for a moment… ah, yes, *your son.*"

"What?" she shrieked.

"That's right. We're going to take him with us, but not before we've had some fun with you first."

The tears came, and she staggered against the wall. "No, don't do this. I have money I can give you if you'll promise to leave us alone. Go now, and I won't inform the police."

"You won't get the chance to because… you'll be dead."

"Mummy… Mummy…" Hudson shouted, clearly petrified by the man's threats.

"It's all right, sweetheart, Mummy's not going to allow him to hurt us."

The younger man appeared at the top of the stairs, and the older one passed Hudson sideways towards him.

"Hold him while I get set up. Let's get more comfortable in the main bedroom, shall we?"

"Why? What are you going to make me do?"

The older one wiggled his eyebrows, and her bowels moved.

Don't let me disgrace myself, not in front of them or Hudson. Shit, how am I going to get us out of this?

"Move it. Time is against us, as they say." He picked up the holdall the other man had put on the floor beside him. "You can lead the way, and don't try any funny business."

"My son doesn't have to witness this; it'll kill him to see you hurting me."

"You reckon? I have a different opinion about that."

Bile appeared in her throat, and she couldn't hold it back. She heaved and mumbled, "I'm going to be sick, please, don't do this in front of my son."

"What you want no longer matters, love. Get in the bedroom or we'll hurt your son."

She held out a hand and pleaded, "No, look at him, he's scared, don't hurt him, I'm begging you. You have my permission to do what you like to me, but please, not in front of Hudson, and please... please... don't hurt him, he's only five. He's too young to witness something like this. God help me!"

"He ain't gonna help you, so you can cut that crap out right away. Get in the bedroom, that's the last time I'm going to tell you."

Reluctantly, Casey moved towards her bedroom, her legs weak and wobbly beneath her. She made it to the bed and sat on the edge to recover from her exertions. Her heart was pounding uncontrollably, affecting her breathing. She clutched a hand to her chest. "I'm having trouble breathing."

"Stop trying to pull the wool over my eyes, it ain't gonna wash, bitch. You own a gym, for fuck's sake, you should be fitter than a butcher's dog." He laughed and faced the other man, taking pride in the joke he'd just cracked.

"I've been ill lately. We were on our way to the hospital. They're supposed to be running some tests on my heart today."

"Really? What's going on with you then?"

"I've been suffering from shortness of breath lately and an irregular heartbeat. I've had to cut back on the stress I've been dealing with over the years."

"Are you winding me up? I know you're planning to open another gym in Whitehaven, it's been all over the local papers. Cutting back on stress, my arse. Doing that is only going to double the strain you're under now." He shot forward and smacked her around the face.

She screamed, and so did Hudson.

"You don't understand, I'm employing someone to run that place for me. It's okay, baby, Mummy isn't hurt, I promise you."

"Stop promising the kid it's going to be all right, when it isn't. Get the chair over and tie the kid to it," ordered the older man.

"Mummy, Mummy, man gonna hurt me."

"It's okay, sweetie, do what he says, we're going to play a special game together. There's nothing to be scared about, trust me, darling."

Hudson's face crinkled, and his mouth formed a straight line, pulling tight across the new teeth he'd cut recently as the tears welled up in his bright-blue eyes.

"Don't cry. Close your eyes and count to fifty. Can you do that for Mummy, sweetheart?"

He nodded, still on the verge of tears, but she could make out how hard he was trying to be brave.

"I'll do it… for you… Mummy."

Casey's heart broke, not for what lay ahead of her but for what her only child was about to go through at the hands of these monsters. "Get on with it," she mouthed at the older man.

He rubbed his hands together and then reached into the bag.

Her intestines twisted themselves into the tightest of knots, and her hands shook uncontrollably as her fear escalated. She watched, holding her breath, waiting to see what he was about to pull out of his holdall.

When he withdrew a large knife with a serrated blade, she thought she was going to vomit. He held the handle out for her to take.

"Don't try any funny business. Hold the knife in your right hand."

She stared at him, confused. "And do what with it?" she whispered in case Hudson overheard the conversation.

Her son was counting loudly and had only reached the mid-teens.

The older man leaned in and whispered, "I want you to slice your wrist, wide open, don't hold back."

Casey sucked in a large breath and shook her head vigorously. "I won't do it, I can't. Why would you even want me to do such a vile thing? Why?"

"What's that saying? Ask me no questions and I'll tell you no lies."

She found his grin unnerving. "I've never heard that before," she lied and gulped noisily.

"I don't believe you."

"What can I say? You're obviously more educated than me."

"I like you; it's a shame I won't get to know you. Now do it, slit your fucking wrist or I'll use the knife and cut your fucking kid's throat, and believe me, I'll have no regrets doing it."

"Why?"

He cleared his throat and said, "Because I can. Think of me as the person to make you slow down."

"What? Slow down? Why would I want to slow down?"

"Because being a workaholic puts your family at risk, as it has today."

"That doesn't make sense. I have to work, how else am I going to look after Hudson? He understands why I have a career. He never complains because he's used to it."

"Kids shouldn't have to 'get used to it'. A mother's place is in the home, caring for the kids she gave birth to, otherwise, why have them?"

"That statement is old-fashioned and no longer has a place in today's society."

"Old-fashioned, is it? Still, I suppose I expected that from you. I'm wasting my time here. Let's get on with your punishment, we haven't got long left."

By this time, Hudson was up to thirty-one and showing no signs of slowing down. Tears dripped onto her cheeks, the love for her son overwhelming her, blocking out any thoughts of fear she had before. Resigned to her fate, she again told her captors to get on with it.

"Hey, do I have to remind you that you're the one holding all the cards as well as the knife?" The older one laughed, but not loud enough to disturb her son.

"I can't do it, I don't have the courage to take my own life. I've never agreed when people deem committing suicide is the coward's way out. It's not, it takes guts, guts I don't appear to have right now."

He grabbed her by the scruff of the neck and thumped his

forehead against hers a couple of times. "Selfish to the end, that's what you are. You've got the opportunity to do this, to save your son, and still you choose not to. Adam, let's get this over with, you can kill the boy. Get the knife."

"No, no, I won't let you kill him. Don't do this, he's a child, he has the rest of his life ahead of him. Why rob him of that?"

"You know what the fucking answer is, so do it," he sneered. "My patience is teetering on the edge. One more refusal from you, and I'm warning you, Adam will do the deed."

With her options running out, Casey's hands shook violently when she placed the tip of the blade on her wrist. She paused, summing up the courage to complete the vile task, resisting the temptation to thrust the knife into the man's gut. Her courage, what she had left of it, seeped away into oblivion. She sliced through her wrist, the pain excruciating, and she sobbed. "I can't do it… Don't make me do this."

"Give me the knife."

Tears misted her vision. She stared at the man and shook her head then thrust the knife at him. The attack surprised her. She didn't even realise what she was doing until it was too late. The knife pierced his side.

"What the fuck…? That's it. Your stupidity has signed your son's death warrant as well as your own, dumb bitch." He wrestled the knife out of her hand but not before catching his palm a few times on the serrated edges. He slapped her around the face. Her head snapped to the right and then to the left, the force making her neck click several times.

"I'm not ready to die and I will fight with every breath left in my body."

"Putting your son's life in danger? Or had you forgotten that part?"

"I'm not, I'm trying to secure both of our futures. There must be something I can give you rather than you do this to us, there has to be. Name your price, my business, this house. Material things mean nothing to me, but don't take my son away from me, please?"

He clapped her. "What a speech that was, worthy of an Oscar. Sadly, it changes nothing. I'm giving you one last chance to do the right thing: end this before it gets messy." He turned to face her son, who by now had reached forty-two.

She shook her head. "This is so unfair. How can you stand there and expect me to take my own life like this? What have I ever done to you? Do I know you? I don't recognise your face."

"No, you don't. Get on with it. You've got seven seconds left before Hudson brings the curtain down on both your lives. Six, five, four, three…"

The metallic smell of the blood filled her nostrils, and fear suffocated her breathing as he returned the knife to her trembling hand. *Two, one…* She lost control of all her senses and plunged the knife into her stomach. Her eyes flickered closed; she struggled to keep them open. Her last thoughts were of her son, screaming for her.

Mummy… I want my mummy…

CHAPTER 7

Sam felt like she'd been hit by ten lorries in a mile-long collision on the M1 when she heard the news on the car radio the following morning on the drive into work. She lashed out at the steering wheel.

Another death of a young woman, an extremely successful woman, by all accounts. Are they connected? Both deaths staged to look like they were suicides? Or am I guilty of overthinking things?

Bob met her in the car park.

"Morning, I've just heard the news. Do you want to head over there straight away?"

"Yep, I think we should." He jumped in the passenger seat and entered the address they'd been given in the satnav. "I can't believe we've got another one."

She selected Drive and left the car park.

"Are you sure?" he asked, "or is that your assumption?"

"Call it women's intuition."

"Did you have to? You know I can't stand it when you call it that."

Sam sniggered. "I know, that's why I say it."

. . .

When they arrived, they found Des at his vehicle fetching some of his equipment. "Glad you're here."

"I take it we need to get suited up?"

"Of course. I don't want to say much, I'd like to get your thoughts on the scene first."

That's unusual. He doesn't generally ask for my opinion in these circumstances, so why this time?

Sam and Bob slipped on their protective suits and waited for Des to finish collecting his equipment.

"Do you need a hand?" Bob asked.

"I thought you'd never ask. Can you bring those two bags?" Des pointed to the ones he meant and walked towards the house. "She's around the back, just like the one yesterday."

Sam cocked her eyebrow at Bob as if to say, 'I told you so'.

Bob tutted and mumbled something indecipherable under his breath.

Sam examined her surroundings and came to what she thought was a vital conclusion: again, the house was isolated. The property was made of stone. It was hard to tell if it was built centuries ago or was a recent replica, an unusual design all the same. The feature that really caught her eye was the round turret at one end, which made her mind up about its authenticity. "Anyone know what this place used to be? I'm sensing it probably had an important use in the past."

"It might have been a mill. Perhaps the blades, or whatever you call them, were removed at one time," Bob suggested.

"I know them as sails," Des chipped in. "But I've heard others call them blades, so you might be right. The turret played a significant role in the woman's death. That's all I'm saying, for now."

"Shit!" Sam muttered, her mind racing.

They wandered down the side of the building. The

grounds were beautiful, they could have been plucked from the pages of any gardening magazine, a possible article highlighting a stately home. "Jesus, from the road, you wouldn't think all this was back here, would you?"

"It's breathtaking, and I'm not usually keen on gardens," Bob agreed. "Can you imagine the hours of work that have gone into creating something as magnificent as this?"

"I dread to think. I reckon there are decades of work here, not just a few hours here and there every week. There must be a resident gardener on site at all times."

"Can we get on?" Des sounded bored. "And you've probably nailed it with your assumption. It was the gardener who found the body."

"Damn, where is he?"

"Sitting in his car, around the front. I told him you'd be wanting a word with him. Shall we get on?"

"Get out of bed early, did you, grumpy old man?" Sam said before realising who she was speaking to.

"I didn't and I'm not. This is me being in professional mode, and so should you be, both of you."

Sam pulled a face behind his back. "That told us," she said to her partner out of the side of her mouth.

Bob grinned.

They reached the back of the vast residence, and were confronted with the body of the victim. A woman in her early thirties. She was naked, which struck Sam as odd because the first victim had been fully clothed when they'd discovered her body.

"Why naked?" she asked.

"No idea," Des replied. "I thought it was odd, too, given where she was found."

"Outside?" Sam queried, if that's what he meant.

Des glanced up and pointed. "No, I believe she came from

up there, from the turret. Would someone really think about throwing themselves from there if they were naked?"

"It takes all sorts," Sam said. However, his observation sparked a thought. "What's the cause of death, can you tell us yet?"

"Another woman who has cuts to her wrist, but I believe they are superficial. She also has a significant wound to her abdomen which is possibly what resulted in her death, but maybe not."

Sam frowned and glanced at the woman's wounds, what she could see of them, without getting permission from Des to get any closer. "I can see the wound on one wrist." Sam took a couple of steps forward and her gaze was drawn to the amount of blood covering the woman's stomach and the ground beneath the wound. "Ouch, yes, a gaping hole likely to cause a lot of damage."

"Understatement of the year," Bob chided.

"All right, I was talking openly, stating my observations out loud rather than internally. The angles of her limbs are conducive with a fall from a great height, aren't they?"

"Correct," Des replied. "Anything else?"

Sam stared at the victim for a few moments longer and then shook her head. "I can't see anything. What am I missing?"

"The bruising that is developing on her back, there's definitely a handprint there."

Sam rubbed her hand around her chin. "Suggesting that she was pushed, before or after the other injuries occurred?"

"I need to take a look at what the techs have found inside the house before I commit further. Do you want to do that now?"

"I don't mind. Would it not be better to deal with the body out here first?"

Des stared at her. "Why? Do you think she's going to rise up from the dead and run off?"

"Sorry, I didn't make myself clear. What I was getting at is, don't you think we should cover her body?"

"All in good time. I don't want to contaminate the scene by throwing a sheet over her."

Sam shrugged, sensing she was going to lose this particular argument with the pathologist. "Okay, you're in charge with regard to the body. Lead the way."

Des did just that. They followed him into the neatly decorated grand hallway.

"Nothing to see around here, I'm eager to get upstairs," Sam said.

"So am I," Bob agreed.

Des walked ahead of them. "Trevor, are you here?"

"Up at the top of the turret. There are thirty steps to climb."

"That'll keep us fit, save us going to the gym," Bob quipped, earning himself a jab in the side from Sam's elbow.

"Ouch."

They reached the landing then walked the length of the hallway to an open doorway at the end and climbed the concrete winding stairs that led them onto the roof of the turret. It was a snug fit for the four of them. Trevor was firing off shots of the area with his camera then angled his long lens on the scene below, to where the deceased's body lay horizontally on the grass verge.

"Any sign that she put up a fight? Did she climb through the raised stonework?" Sam couldn't imagine squeezing through a gap that tiny, and she was a similar size to the victim.

"Nothing up here, well, apart from the odd drop of blood." He pointed to the areas which they had avoided when they had joined Trevor in the turret. "There are also some splashes on top of the 'raised stonework' but not on the sides."

Sam recoiled at his words. "So, what are you saying? That whoever killed her picked her up and launched her over the edge?"

"Judging by the trajectory," Des said. "If she had thrown herself off, I think she would have landed closer to the building."

Sam slowly nodded as she considered Des' scenario. "It makes sense. Anything else up here for us?"

"No, that's it. You might want to take a look in the main bedroom next," Trevor said. He waited until the area was clear and returned to his task.

Des accompanied Sam and Bob to the bedroom.

She peered over the pathologist's shoulder the moment he entered the room and cursed under her breath. "Shit! What the fuck?"

There was a long trail of blood coming towards the doorway, and the cover of the quilt had a large patch of blood at the edge. The three of them approached the bed in silence, each of them consumed by their thoughts.

"Fuck," Bob muttered. "So, she was killed here and dragged upstairs?" He glanced over his shoulder at the door. "Correction, there's no sign of any drag marks, so the killer must have carried her."

"Or killers," Sam added. "To carry the victim, who, let's face it, might still have been alive at the time, all the way from here, up that long landing then up thirty steep steps, the person would have to be strong, wouldn't they?"

"The woman was quite small, however it does seem logical to assume the murder was carried out by two killers," Des confirmed.

"Looking back at the first victim, could the same be said about that crime scene?" Sam was trying to fit the pieces of the puzzle together, the only way she knew how, using her logic and experience.

"I can't really say, not off the top of my head. You were there, at the location, what do you think?"

Sam cast her mind back to the scene at Gabby Addis' house. Her eyes narrowed as she mentally assessed the bedroom and what they perceived had happened in that room. "Hmm... well, there's also the missing boy to be considered. Someone would have needed to have kept him under control while the killer murdered his mother unless he was tied up." Her gaze flicked around the room, another important thought striking her. She walked over to the bed and with her gloved hand, she picked up the silver frame. In it was a picture of the deceased and a child. "Bugger, look at this." She carried it back to Des and Bob to show them. "It seems likely this was her child. Another possible comparison to the Addis' case."

"Want me to check the other bedrooms?" Bob said. He took off before Sam had the chance to respond. He reappeared in the doorway a few moments later. "Yep, we've got a young boy's bedroom next door."

"What state is the room in? Is it tidy?"

"As far as I could tell. Do you want me to go back and make a thorough assessment?"

"No, I'll do it."

From the doorway, Bob indicated which room it was. Sam pushed open the door, and something felt immediately off to her. She searched the wardrobe; there were a few clothes in there but not that many, making her wonder if someone had taken the majority of the boy's clothes. Sam strode across the room to check the drawers. "Half-empty. A couple of them aren't closed properly, either."

"Are you thinking along the lines that we have another child abduction on our hands?" Bob asked from the doorway.

"I'm not sure, but it does seem strange. We need to get some patrols out here, to search the grounds, just in case the mother told the boy to run and he's hiding out there. I also need to have a chat with the gardener, see what his take is on everything."

"I agree. I'll give the station a call, get the reinforcements actioned."

Sam stood in the centre of the room, visualising what might have taken place.

Was the boy locked in here while the killers did away with his mother? Or did they do the unthinkable, make the child watch his mother being killed? Maybe they tortured the mother and the child. Are they the type to get off on doing that? Either way, there's another boy involved, possibly abducted and absolutely no evidence for us to go on, as yet. Has the killer taken both boys? Are they being held somewhere or are they being abducted to order? To be sold to the highest bidder, either here or abroad?

"I said are you okay, Sam?" Des touched her forearm, startling her.

"Sorry, I was in a world of my own, contemplating what the possibilities are surrounding the two boys."

He raised a hand. "Hey, that wouldn't be you jumping the gun now, would it? For all we know, the boy might be elsewhere, at school perhaps or staying with his other parent."

"That's true. You're right, I must stick to the facts at our disposal, for now. I'll have a word with the gardener, see what he has to say."

"Let me know as soon as you can, will you?"

"I will."

Sam and Bob walked back downstairs, through the house, stopping periodically as they reached a new, undiscovered room. Sam poked her head in to check if there was anything out of place. There wasn't. Until they came to the kitchen, or rather, the utility room. She spotted the washing machine had been switched on and was flashing, indicating that it had come to the end of its cycle, but she also noticed a wrench lying on the floor, sticking out from underneath the dirty washing, waiting to go in the machine. "What do you make of that?"

Bob shrugged. "It's a wrench? Maybe she had a problem with the plumbing and fetched it to have a go at it herself rather than call someone in. Perhaps she was a keen DIYer; it's not unheard of for women to turn their hand to those sorts of things these days."

Sam ran a hand around her face. "Still seems odd to me, there's nothing else out of place around the house, you've seen that for yourself, and yet in here…"

"I think you're reading more into it than you should be. Do you want me to get one of the techs to bag it and test it, just in case?"

"Yeah, I think it would be remiss of us to ignore it."

Bob huffed out a breath and left the room. He returned with a tech who bagged the wrench.

"I'll see if there is anything else in here," the tech said.

Sam thanked the tech, then she and Bob passed through the kitchen and exited the back door. They approached the older man, sitting in his white van. The signwriting on the side of it told her it belonged to Frank Inman, professional garden designer.

He saw them walking towards him and jumped out. "Hello, are you the officer in charge?"

"I am. DI Sam Cobbs, and this is my partner, DS Bob Jones, and you're Frank Inman, I presume?"

"That's right. I was the one who found her. I rang nine-nine-nine immediately. It was such a shock… seeing her like that."

"Are you up to answering a few questions, Frank?"

"Of course. I've just had a strong cup of tea. Always makes you feel better, doesn't it?"

"It does. Why don't we take a seat over here?" Sam led the way to the table and chairs situated on the edge of the lawn.

Bob withdrew his notebook and sat beside her while Frank took the seat opposite them.

"Can you tell us what time you arrived?" Sam asked.

"I was early today. Casey, I mean Miss Pardoe, had an appointment at the hospital, and she asked me to drop by earlier than normal because she wanted to discuss the plans I had drawn up for the latest idea she had for landscaping the side garden."

"Have you worked here long?"

He spread his arm out behind him and said, "All of this is down to me. I've been coming here for decades, and my particulars got passed on by the previous owners." He shook his head. "In all my days… I've never come across anything like this before."

"I'm sorry you had to witness this today. Can you tell us when you saw Casey last?"

"I spoke to her on the phone yesterday, around lunchtime, to check if today was still on."

"And how did she sound to you?"

"Her usual cheerful self. I've never known her to be anything else, if I'm honest with you. I can't figure it out whether she jumped or what. She wouldn't end up with a wound like that in her stomach, would she? Not that I got close enough to see where the blood was coming from, you know, what with her being naked."

"The pathologist will need to make a thorough examination before he puts his neck on the line and informs us of the cause of death. When you arrived, or during the drive here, did you pass any other vehicles?"

"No, there was nothing here, and I don't recall seeing

anything on the road, either. May I ask why? You're not suggesting someone did this to her, are you?"

Sam shrugged. "No, I'm not implying that, but it's important we ask these sorts of questions right from the word go."

"Ah, yes, of course. I understand now. She was so happy about opening the second gym, even tried to sign me up to it before it was scheduled to open because I live closer to Whitehaven than Workington. I got my son to join, he's really keen on all that stuff, whereas a morning's work in the garden is like a session in the gym for me some days."

"I can imagine. Do you happen to know the name of her gym?"

"I do, I thought it was a strange name, but then I got to thinking about it and really liked it. It's called Weightless not Clueless."

Sam chewed on her lip, agreeing with his perception that the name was very strange indeed. "I don't get it, but that's not uncommon with some of the names being chosen by businesses these days."

"Yeah, they are a bit weird, I have to agree. What's wrong with people using their names? I've always done it, and my business has gone from strength to strength over the years."

"If this is all down to you, I'm not surprised you are in demand. We admired the garden when we got here."

His cheeks reddened. "Thank you, that means a lot. I've always taken pride in my work."

"It shows. I don't suppose you happen to know much about Casey's personal life, do you?"

"I'm not one to gossip. What she tells me has never been repeated elsewhere; she knew she could trust me."

"I'm sure. We saw photos of her with a child. Did she have custody of him?"

"Oh, heck. Little Hudson, yes, he lives here with her. I'm guilty of not giving the child a thought, my priority was with calling you lot. Once a patrol turned up, they told me to sit in my van. No, that's a lie, sorry, it wasn't until the man in the white van arrived. He was the one who told me you'd want a word with me."

"That was the pathologist. I take it you haven't seen Hudson since you got here?"

"No. The back door was unlocked, but that was normal. Casey tended to leave it like that for me when she was out, always telling me to help myself to a cuppa in her absence. But I haven't been inside the house since I got here. It's taken everything I've got not to vomit; the urge was there when I found her, I can tell you. I've never come across a dead person before, let alone someone I know, apart from my wife, but that's a different story. Casey was really nice. Even though she lived in a grand house like this, she never, ever looked down her nose at me. I'll genuinely miss her. She always gave me a gift at Christmas, none of my other clients do that. Plus, last year she made a huge fuss over me for my birthday. Quite embarrassed, I was. I let it slip the week before that I would be spending it on my own as my wife had recently passed away and my son had other plans on that day, and she laid on a garden party for the three of us, me, her and Hudson. The little chap loved it as much as I did. I remember him being so excited for hours."

"Sorry to hear of your wife's passing. Was she ill?"

"She wasn't until she got taken in for an operation on her hip. While she was recovering in hospital, she picked up four different infections. The final one, sepsis, was the one that eventually killed her. I'm still in the process of suing them; my solicitor said my case is in a queue. Bloody NHS has gone to pot over the years, I wouldn't want an overnight stay in hospital if anything ever happened to me. I've heard some real horror stories lately, and not just about the hospitals around here, either."

"It is an unfortunate position we find ourselves in. My other half is in hospital at the moment. I have to say, that so far, he's been treated exceptionally well by the staff."

"Keep a watchful eye on things. I thought the same when Eileen was in there, but then things declined rapidly." He teared up and angrily swiped at his eyes. "Damn, I thought I was done crying about this. I'm sorry, I guess it's still very raw. It's the guilt I have to live with. She was desperate to get out of hospital after hearing so many horror stories from some of the patients, but I was the one who encouraged her to stay in there an extra few days and… she never came home again. I have to live with that guilt for the rest of my life."

Sam rested a hand over his. "You mustn't blame yourself. I'm a true believer that when our time is up, there's very little we can do to prevent our deaths."

"Maybe. I've never really thought about it before. Still, you're not here to listen to my drivel. I'm so sorry for burdening you with my tales of woe."

"A problem shared and all that. It's probably the shock of seeing Casey lying there that has stirred up your grief again."

His head dipped. "You're not wrong there. They were very much alike, Casey and Eileen, both independent women. My wife ran a shoe shop in her younger days. She raised my son and worked full-time. I admit I was worse than useless, I think most men were in those days. The child-rearing aspect of a marriage was always taken on by the wives. I've had a chance to look back over the years, since her death, and have many regrets, I can tell you. You women amaze the hell out of me, the way you handle everyday life. It's much harder for men to accept their role in the family, or maybe I'm the only one guilty of that."

"You're not," Bob said. "I tend to leave all that kind of stuff to my wife, too, and still manage to give her a rough ride when she has the audacity to complain about something."

Sam narrowed her eyes at her partner; this was all new to her. He had the decency to look embarrassed and stare at his notebook.

"I'm sure you did your part in the marriage, Frank. You mustn't have regrets, it's not going to do any good at the end of the day, is it?"

"No, that's what my son says. He tells me I'm being foolish, but the guilt is always there, eating away at you. It's true what they say, hindsight is a wonderful thing."

She didn't want to rush the man, felt he needed to unburden himself, and what better way to do that than with a stranger, who wasn't likely to judge him? But on the other hand, they had an investigation they needed to get to grips with. Reluctantly, she said, "Did Casey have any family in the area? A partner perhaps? I take it she wasn't married, not if you call her Miss Pardoe."

"No, she got rid of her fella a couple of years ago. Good riddance to him, too. Dreadful human being, he was. Got my back up on more than one occasion. He's a builder and was always spouting his mouth off, offering advice that wasn't needed when I brought the digger out back here. It was around that time the arguments started. I pulled up one day and saw him chasing her and the child around the patio at the side. I shouted at him to leave them alone. I shouldn't have interfered, but any real man would have done the same in my position. His face was contorted with rage. Christ knows what would have happened to her and the kid if I hadn't shown up when I did. He told me to do one, to stop butting my nose into their business. Damn idiot, he had no idea how to treat a woman. She deserved better than him. He was the lowest of the low, in my opinion. An utter tosspot."

"Is he a local chap?" Sam asked, her intrigue rising.

"Yeah, Twathead, I like to call him. I've heard unsavoury

reports about his building work from several of my clients who have had the misfortune of using him over the years."

"Apart from Twathead, does he go by another name?" Sam did her best to suppress the smile threatening to emerge. She liked this man, found him easy-going.

"Sorry, that was rude of me to even say it. Yes, it's Kevin Davis. He says he's a professional builder, but that's debatable at times. Mouth almighty who treated Casey appallingly. I didn't really see it until I caught him chasing her around that day. I kept my eye on him after that, made sure I was always working within a few feet of them, until Casey eventually saw him for what he was and kicked him to the kerb."

"So, you'd class it as a turbulent relationship then?"

"Yes. The more I thought about it, the more I put it down to him being jealous."

Sam tilted her head. "Jealous of another man vying for her attention?"

"Yep, that's what it seemed like to me, even though I had no feelings for the woman, other than treating her well as a client. Blimey, she was young enough to be my daughter."

"We'll check him out. Has he been around lately?"

"No, I've not had the misfortune of seeing him for over two years or more. Not since she kicked him out. He doesn't even come back to visit his son."

This news spiked Sam's interest. "Hudson is his son?"

"That's right. Casey was amazing, how she dealt with the breakup. I think at one time the police had to be called to escort him off the premises. He was spouting nonsense that he had a right to live here. She told me he contributed zilch to the running costs of this place, and yet he expected her to sell it and give him half. Like I said, he's a prime Twathead. I'd call him worse than that if you weren't present. There are some people in this life who you know deserve a good slap now and then to keep them in check—he's one of them. Can't stand men like that, treating women the way they do. Makes me sick to the stomach."

"I can tell how angry he made you feel. Had Casey mentioned if he's called her recently? Been pestering her at all?"

"No, if he had, she didn't say anything to me. Honestly, she's been so wrapped up in the new launch, bubbling with excitement for months, making sure everything went according to plan. Only last week she told me she couldn't believe how obliging the builders had been during the renovations, compared to the reports she'd heard about Twathead." He shuddered. "Just thinking about that bloke turns my stomach. Ties it into knots, it does. If I were you, and if you're going to class this as a suspicious death, he'd be right at the top of my list, not that I'm trying to tell you how to do your job, far from it. But something ain't sitting right with me; she was so happy, even during our conversation yesterday. When she told me she had an appointment at the hospital, she was still very upbeat. A woman who was enjoying her life and looking forward to what it held in the future. I can't believe her life has ended this way; it just doesn't make sense to me."

"I promise we'll get to the bottom of it. Do you know if there have been any strangers on the property lately? Any workmen here perhaps, as well as at the gym?"

"No, only me. She always maintained that she could trust me explicitly, and she was right, too. I thought of her as family but still kept a safe distance, if you get where I'm coming from? I've never thought it right getting too close to my clients, although I did treat her differently because I had so much admiration for what she had accomplished and was about to achieve with the new gym opening. And another thing to note down in that book of yours, I never once heard her raise her voice at that child. He was perfect in my eyes, always happy, never pushed the boundaries like some kids can do. I wonder where he is."

"That's what we're desperate to find out. Going back to a question I asked earlier, does she have any family in the area?"

"Sorry, yes, I went off the subject, didn't I? Ranting on about Twathead. What I should have told you is that her parents live up near Carlisle. You'll be testing me to come up with their names."

"It's okay, we can do the necessary research. Is their surname also Pardoe?"

"Yes, I seem to recall Casey telling me that they were in the legal business. Maybe solicitors." He paused to think for a moment and shook his head. "No, I'm wrong, I believe the father is a judge."

Sam's heart sank at the prospect of having to break the news to the couple in person. "Bob, can you get the team on it right away?"

Bob left the table and moved away from them to call the station.

In his absence, Sam took a moment to check if Frank was okay. "How are you holding up?"

He ran a hand through his hair. "I'm devastated. I know it might come across as me being all right, but I'm determined not to crumble. My biggest wish now is to do all I can to help you with your investigation. I can't do that if I'm a sobbing wreck, can I? She was truly in a class of her own, and I will miss her dearly. But my thoughts remain with her son and what might have happened to him."

"I understand your concern. Try not to worry about him. We've got patrols on the way. They'll conduct a thorough search when they get here."

"I don't think I'll ever be able to get that image out of my head. I hope it's not the first thing I conjure up when I think of her, I won't be able to live with that."

"I can understand you thinking that way. Maybe you should see a counsellor if things get tough. Are you going to be all right to drive home? Do you want me to give your son a call, see if he will come and pick you up?"

"No, he's away for a few days attending his best friend's stag do. I'll be fine." He held up his hand to check his composure. "At least I've stopped shaking now."

Sam smiled. "It's okay for men to be upset, you know. You men always feel that women will judge you—we don't. I know that's hard for some men to fathom."

"I'm not like that, don't worry about me, Inspector. Just promise me you'll find the bastard who did this and do all you can to find where Hudson is. That's what is getting to me right now, the fact that Hudson's welfare slipped my mind. It should have been my first consideration; instead, I just froze, well, after I called the police."

Sam laid a hand over his. "Please, stop punishing yourself, you did the right thing. You were close to the victim, that will be a contributing factor in the way you process what's gone on. You haven't done anything wrong, quite the opposite, in fact. So please, give yourself a break."

"Easier said than done, eh? I'd like to hang around and search for the boy. Will I be allowed to do that?"

She squeezed his hand and then let it go. "As much as we'd love you to stay here with us, I think it will be better if you went home, left us to deal with the search."

"In other words, you think I'll get in the way?"

"No, not at all. I just think it'll be easier on you if you aren't involved. It can be an extremely emotional exercise, even for our guys, let alone someone who knows him as well as you do."

"Oh God, are you saying that you think he might be dead… like his mother?"

"No, I'm not. But the more we search and the result turns out to be negative, the more upset you're likely to become, and I can assure you, it's around that time that the frustration tends to kick in, along with a whole host of other emotions."

"Okay, I'll take your advice and go home."

"Good, it's for the best. Can you give me your address? We'll need to take a statement over the next few days, if that's okay with you?"

"Yes, or do you want me to pop down the station later?"

"Whichever suits you, if you think you'll be up to it."

"I'd like to get it out of the way, not that I'm likely to forget any of the facts."

"I wish everyone thought that way."

Bob rejoined them.

"Any luck?" Sam asked.

At first, he seemed a little hesitant to speak in front of Frank. Sam nodded, letting her partner know it was okay.

"Yep, we've managed to track them down, but they're on holiday in Portugal at the moment."

"Shit! Sorry, excuse my French. That's not ideal."

"Damn, yes, I remember Casey telling me that they were going away last weekend." Frank winced. "They're staying in a friend's villa over there. I'm sure Casey wrote the number down and pinned it up on the noticeboard in the kitchen while her mother was on the phone. Casey and I were going over some ideas when her mother rang to share the news."

"See, I'm glad you're still with us, Frank. If you weren't, we'd be scrabbling around for the information for hours, if not days."

"I'm glad I could help in some small way. I've felt totally useless up until now."

"Nonsense. Our being here is down to you. Right, thank you so much for all your help. We're going to need to get back to it now. As soon as we've found that number, we'll need to contact the parents."

Frank rose from his seat. "I don't envy you. I'll drop by the station at around three, if that's okay?"

"I'll let the desk sergeant know. He'll make sure an officer is on hand to meet with you. Thanks for all you've done for us today. Sorry we had to meet under these circumstances."

He stuck his hand in his pocket and withdrew a card. "If you know anyone who needs a garden makeover, will you pass on my details to them? I'll be on the lookout for extra work what with this place now being off the agenda."

"I'll be sure to do that, Frank. Take care of yourself."

"I'll be fine. Hope all goes well with the investigation. Do your best to find the boy, won't you?"

"Absolutely. I'll let you know, if and when, we find the little chap."

"I'd appreciate it. Thanks."

She watched him walk away from them, sensing his disposition was a touch better than when they'd first met. "Nice chap, I feel for him. I reckon he was really close to Casey, treated her more like a member of his family than a client. He's really worried about the boy, too."

"Aren't we all? The patrols are a few minutes away. Do you want to go back inside, see if we can find the number for the villa?"

"You read my mind. God, I'm not looking forward to speaking to the parents, but needs must."

They headed towards the back door. Sam tried to picture passing a corkboard on the way through the house, but she couldn't place it. Bob entered the doorway and led the way through the kitchen.

"There, in the corner, just past the fridge."

"Ah, yes, it's tucked away out of sight. Explains why I couldn't recall it."

They wandered across the room. The back door opened behind them, and Des joined them.

"What's going on? Did you have a chat with the gardener? I thought you were going to report back to me with your findings."

"Sorry, we've only just finished interviewing him. He gave us some information about where the victim's parents are staying. Thought we'd check it out first and then I was going to come and find you."

"Likely story. What about the child, did the gardener have any clues about him?"

"Nothing, he was beside himself. Told us he's a good kid who adores his mother. Backup should be arriving soon. I'll issue them with their instructions before I give the parents a call."

"Here it is," Bob said behind her, handing her the note.

Relief hit Sam, but it quickly turned to dread as she reflected on the task ahead of her. "How are you getting on outside, Des?"

"I needed to take a break; you won't hear me say those words too often, either. Poor woman. I believe the wounds to her wrists were self-inflicted, but something is telling me the cuts were possibly made under duress. Don't ask me how I know that, will you? I have no scientific proof to offer you."

"It doesn't matter, I rely on gut instinct a lot. It's finding the evidence to back up those claims that can often be a bugbear for us. The gardener couldn't praise the woman enough. She ran a successful gym business and was in the process of opening a second one in Whitehaven. He told me she had everything to live for, so there's no way I'd be willing to consider this as a suicide."

"It's not. I can categorically tell you that now. You saw the blood trails upstairs, from the main bedroom to the turret. That alone points to her being thrown from the building, as opposed to jumping. I've checked the property from the outside, can't see any sign of cameras out there. I was on my way in here to see if there were any inside. I don't recall spotting any on the walk-through before, do you?"

Sam tutted. "No, the thought hadn't crossed my mind until now. That's another similarity to the first case. No security present. Does that mean that's a key priority for the killers? Or does kidnapping the kids rank highly on their agenda? Why choose single-parent families? What about the women both being professionals at the top of their game? Could that be a significant factor?"

"I'd say all of the aforementioned," Des agreed. "Plus, the fact that the killers clean up after themselves, no sign of any weapons lying around at either scene, from what I can tell."

Sam held up a finger. "I have to disagree. We found a wrench in the utility room that seemed to be out of place. One of the techs has bagged it up."

"Interesting. I'll make sure they treat it as a priority when we return to the lab. Anything else I should know?"

"Isn't that enough?"

He grinned. "Between us, I believe we've done well, so far. I'm going to get Ray to take the photos needed and then get the body transferred to the mortuary. All being well, I should have the PM results for you by the end of the day."

"Great. Are we definitely linking the two crimes now?"

"I think we should. It would be a huge mistake for us not to."

He turned and walked out of the back door.

Sam stared at the number on the slip of paper. She took a few minutes to mull over how she should tell the parents their daughter was dead and, furthermore, how she was going to broach the subject about their grandchild being missing. She despised making these types of calls over the phone. Had they been holidaying in this country, Sam would have rung the local nick where they were staying and asked an officer on duty to do the deed.

"I wish I could jump on a flight and tell the parents in person."

"It's not practical, not when you have two, no, make it three, investigations on the go."

"Three? Shit, yes, you're right, I'd forgotten all about Rhys' assault. Shame on me."

"Yes, shame on you. I won't drop you in it, your secret's safe with me."

Sam's mind drifted to the hospital and the note she had found under Rhys' body.

"Hey, there you go again, drifting off. What's going on, Sam? This isn't like you. Spill!"

"There's something niggling me about the note the attacker left at the hospital." She withdrew her phone from her pocket and hunted for the photo of the note. "He was goading me, telling me not to judge a book by its cover. What if...?"

"Don't leave me hanging. What if, what?"

"What if attacking Rhys was done on purpose?"

"Of course it was."

She huffed out a breath, annoyed that her partner wasn't on board with her thought process. "On purpose *to cause a distraction?*"

"What the fuck? Are you telling me you think the murders could be connected with the attack on Rhys?"

"I'm not sure, maybe. Ordinarily, I wouldn't be so quick to jump in with such a bizarre idea, but that note is making me reconsider, making my head spin."

"I can't see it myself."

"Okay, maybe I'm talking shit. I suppose we won't know for sure until we have the results from the note."

"Jesus, if you're right... that could open up a whole different can of worms, couldn't it?"

Sam took a moment to reread the note and then slid her phone across the table for Bob to read again. "The more I read it, the more it's triggering the cogs to turn. As I said before, I feel mortified that Rhys has been attacked because of his involvement with me. What kind of warped person does that?"

Bob ran his finger over the phone. "It says here that you've had dealings with the attacker's father. The first thing we need to do is try and figure out who that is."

"The team are working on that aspect back at the station."

"Correction," Bob said. "They're working on so many different angles at the moment to do with the first murder case..."

"You're suggesting we've dropped the ball on Rhys' case?"

Bob raised an eyebrow. "Guilty, without meaning to be. If all three cases are connected, this lead should be our priority, shouldn't it?"

"Most definitely. He's succeeded in doing what he set out to achieve... to cause a distraction. He's been toying with us from the word go, laughing at us. Brazenly visiting Rhys in hospital before he contemplated going off to his next murder. Makes me wonder what else he has up his sleeve for me, for us."

"We need to get back to basics, like you always say, sift through evidence that has been offered to us on a plate. It's all in that note. We're both guilty of being wrapped up in being concerned about Rhys to realise what the perp was up to."

"Bugger, now I'm seething. Not an ideal state to be in when giving the parents a call."

"Ha, I'd say it was perfect timing."

Sam stared at him and then picked up her phone, intending to make the call, only to be disturbed by a loud rap on the back door. Bob leapt out of his chair to answer it, his suit rustling as he sped across the room.

"Not in here, we'll be out shortly." He held up a hand to stress his point to the uniformed officer.

Sam joined them. "I won't be long, Bob." She stepped outside and walked towards the three other officers. "Right, this is what you need to know. We arrived here to find the female owner of the property dead. She was discovered by the gardener. He believes her five-year-old son might have been in the house as the woman was due to set off for an appointment at the hospital this morning; she was intending to take the child with her. Needless to say, the boy was nowhere to be found when we got here. The grounds are vast, with plenty of hiding places for a small child to escape to. We're assuming the mother was killed. What we don't know is what has happened to her son. His name is Hudson. Report back to me personally if you find him."

She dismissed the four officers. They separated to go north, south, east and west across the manicured lawn, in search of the child. Sam watched them disperse with a sinking feeling in her gut that they were all going to come back empty-handed.

"Penny for them?" Bob crept up behind her and asked.

"Jesus, I wish you'd stop doing that when I'm bloody deep in thought. One of these days I'll spin round and give you a karate chop to the neck, or worse still, a knee in the groin. Do I have to remind you where we are? At a murder scene."

"All right. There's no need to go OTT. I apologise, it won't happen again."

"Until the next time." After a moment's pause, she gulped and said, "Sorry, I should be the one apologising, not you. I'm working myself up into a tizzy before I get on the phone to Casey's parents."

"Do you want me to do it?"

Sam smiled, picking up on the reluctance in his tone. "Nice of you to offer, even though deep down you're averse to taking on such tasks."

"You know I wouldn't be able to go through with it… that's why…"

"I know, I'll even finish that sentence for you, shall I? That's why I'm the inspector, am I right?"

He winked and pointed at her. "You've got it. I sense you're keen to delay the chore, are you?"

"Too right I am. God, it's bad enough dropping a bombshell like this to the parents of a deceased in person, it's going to be a hundred times worse having to do it over the phone."

"My heart goes out to you, it really does."

Sam drifted back to the table and chairs on the edge of the lawn, where they had interviewed the gardener. There, she steadied her breathing with a few deep, meaningful breaths. "I don't wish to appear rude, but would you mind making yourself scarce? This is going to be hard enough as it is, without you listening in."

"Charming. Okay, I can take a hint. I'll go and pester Des then."

"You can linger, although I don't want you *pestering* him. The last thing we need is him breathing fire at us about you getting under his feet."

Bob stared at her, shook his head and turned away, mumbling something incoherent as she knew he would.

She rubbed her hands together, her circulation suddenly giving her some gyp. Despite it being the middle of summer, she told herself that some days were chillier than others. This happened to be one of them. Finally, she plucked up the courage to dial the number on the sheet of paper. A man answered the phone.

"This had better be good, I'm enjoying a cocktail in the midday sun over here."

"Hello, sir, sorry to trouble you. Would you be Patrick Pardoe?"

"I would have thought that was obvious. Who are you? And what do you want?"

Sam cleared the lump that had grown in her throat with a cough. "I'm so sorry to disturb you, sir, I wouldn't do, not ordin"

"Stop stuttering and get on with it. First, tell me who you are."

She sucked in a lungful of fresh air and replied, "I'm DI Sam Cobbs of the Cumbria Constabulary."

"What? Has there been a break-in at the house? I haven't had a notification from the alarm company. Mind you, that's nothing new, they're worse than useless, that lot, since they were taken over last year."

"No, it's nothing like that. I need to ask if you're sitting down before I share the news."

An awkward silence filled the line. "Okay, I'm sitting. Now tell me what's going on."

"I'm currently at your daughter Casey's house."

"And? Is she all right? Has something happened to her?" His voice was high-pitched.

"What is it, Patrick? Tell me!" his wife demanded in the background.

"I'm going to put the phone on speaker so my wife can hear this conversation."

"Perhaps that's for the best."

"Go ahead. Why are you at Casey's house? Has something happened either to her or Hudson?"

"It is with regret that I have to tell you that your daughter lost her life this morning."

There was complete silence for a second or two on the other end of the line. Until Mrs Pardoe began weeping.

"Sorry, can you repeat that?" Mr Pardoe said, his voice catching in his throat. "I wasn't sure I heard you correctly."

Sam closed her eyes and tried to hold it together long enough to deliver the devastating news a second time.

"What? What are you telling us? How...? How did she die? It's all right, Ivy. We'll get to the bottom of this."

It was then that Sam realised she had met him in person a few years before. He'd been the presiding judge over a couple of cases she was involved in, which got her thinking. *Shit, is that the connection here? Was Casey punished because her father had something to do with this weirdo or weirdos?*

"I'm sorry for your loss. The gardener called us out to the house this morning. He was the one who found her."

"Did she have a fatal accident? Come on, Inspector, out with it! We need to know the facts, now."

So, she reeled off what had taken place in the last hour and a half. Casey's parents managed to remain silent throughout, allowing her to concentrate on delivering the news professionally, in light of who he was, they were.

"I can't believe what you're telling us. Our daughter was only thirty. Hang on, you haven't mentioned anything about Hudson. Where was he, is he? Did he see her being murd...?"

"We have no way of knowing whether he witnessed the incident or not. Hudson wasn't at the property when we arrived. We have officers on site, checking the extensive grounds around the house, now. As yet, they haven't found him."

Silence, except for Mrs Pardoe's sobbing, filled the line.

"We're going to get on the first plane out of here. Expect us by the end of the day." And he promptly hung up on her.

Sam removed the phone from her ear and placed it on the table beside her. Her gaze wandered to the four different areas of the garden to which the individual officers had gone to conduct their searches for the child. She said a silent prayer for them to find Hudson, even though the knot in her stomach was telling her it was a waste of time conducting the search in the first place. She tucked her phone in her pocket, left her seat and went in search of her partner.

Bob must have heard the crunch of the gravel under her feet as she approached because he turned to face her. "How did it go?"

"Not the best way to tell parents that their only child has been murdered."

She came to an abrupt stop alongside him, and he rubbed her arm.

"I'm sorry you had to deal with that, on top of everything else you have going on at the moment."

"It is what it is. The parents are jumping on the first flight out of there, so don't be surprised if you run into them later, Des. What's happening here?"

"I hope we'll be packed up and out of here long before they arrive. I'd hate for them to see her in this state." The pathologist was crouching, assessing the deceased's wounds again. "Okay, I'm calling it, I think I've seen enough. I'm going to instruct the team to get her transferred to the mortuary."

Sam nodded. She tried to battle through the countless thoughts whistling like a tornado through her mind. "I think we need to get out of here and back to the station. We have a few leads which need investigating. I'd like to get most of those dealt with before the parents descend upon us."

Bob nodded.

"Good luck," Des said and walked away to speak with the

group of techs who had gathered close to the vans. He barked orders at them, and they scattered in various directions.

"Seems like they've succeeded in pissing Des off," Sam said.

"They should know by now he doesn't suffer any form of incompetence. Good on him for having a go at them."

"I'm mentally exhausted," Sam confessed. "We'll stop off at the shop, pick up lunch for the others and thrash out some ideas with the rest of the team when we get back."

"It's unusual for you to admit you're tired, Sam. Do you want to stop off and have a break on the way?"

"I'd love nothing more than to go home, collect Sonny and Casper and take them over to Ennerdale, but it would be totally unprofessional of me. That's not to say the temptation isn't there, though. Walking up there allows me thinking time. I'm sure I'd solve more investigations if I had the lake directly on my doorstep."

Bob chuckled. "Hey, the statistics don't lie, we're still the best team in the area, in case you've forgotten. So, you don't do badly on that front, boss."

"Thanks, I'll take the compliment, coming from you."

They removed their protective clothing and deposited it in the black bag close to the cordon that had been set up. Out of the corner of her eye, she saw one of the uniformed officers come out from the bushes at the end of the lawn.

"I need to check with him before we head off."

"Want me to go? I can sprint over there, if you're too tired."

"Go on then, hurry up, I'm desperate to get back to the station."

CHAPTER 8

The afternoon flew past. When She and Bob got back to the station, Sam handed around the lunch and, after Bob had supplied the team with a coffee, Sam apprised the others of what they had encountered at the house. Then she raised the subject about the note that had been left for her at the hospital.

The team all agreed that it was too much of a coincidence. By the end of the meeting, their to-do list had grown out of control. Sam's personal list appeared to be a foot long. After giving the team their instructions, she went through to her office to tackle her post. However, before she could deal with that, she had something more important on her mind she needed to organise first. A conference. The sooner that was out of the way the better. With two kids now missing and no hint as to what had happened to them, the quicker the news was circulated about their disappearances, the more likely they were to stop the killers in their tracks, if they had any inclination of selling the kids on.

Jackie Penrose, the press officer at the station, told Sam

she had a slot free later that afternoon. They agreed to meet up at four o'clock, which would suit them both. The Pardoes had sent her a text to expect them at around five. Their flight was due to land at two-thirty, and they were planning to drive straight to the station to see her. Holding the conference before they arrived made sense to Sam. After speaking with Jackie, she rang the hospital to check how Rhys was doing. The nurse she had spoken to the day before assured her that he was now on the road to recovery, but the consultant was unwilling to release him too early, which was a relief for Sam to hear. It was one less problem for her to have to deal with. There was no way she'd be able to concentrate properly on the investigations if she knew Rhys was a sitting duck at home.

Leaving her office, she rejoined the rest of the team who had come up with a number of leads in her absence. "What have you got for me?"

Claire was the first to draw her attention. "I've been going over the arrests we've made over the years and created a list of possible connections with the killers. I'm going through it again, crossing off any criminals who have died while they've been locked up."

"Brilliant, thanks, Claire. Can you also check if any of these inmates are due to be released soon? It might be the contributing factor, prompting the killers to make their move. Can you also search for any links the men behind bars might have had with Rhys? I've got it in mind the connection is probably me, but I'd love to be proved wrong."

"I'll crosscheck and see what I can come up with."

"How are we getting on with the CCTV footage around Rhys' building at the time of the attack? Has anything surfaced yet? A vehicle perhaps? Anyone else lingering, watching the attack from a safe distance? Let's revisit the footage with the latest information we have to hand."

"What about the second victim's boyfriend?" Bob asked.

"Can you deal with that for me? Normally, he would be a significant person of interest, however, unless he knew the first victim, I think we'd probably be wasting time going after him."

Bob grimaced and bit his lip.

"Don't you agree with me?" Sam asked.

"I'm not saying I disagree with your suggestion, but I believe it will be wrong of us to dismiss him altogether."

"Okay, carry out the necessary digging, and we'll send a couple of members of the team out to either see him or put him under surveillance. How does that sound to you?"

"Better. I'll get to work on it and report back to you soon."

"Do me a favour, enter his name into the system now, while I'm free, and see what comes up."

Bob pounded the keyboard, and seconds later, Kevin Davis' face filled the screen with a list of minor offences to his name. "Hmm, this makes interesting reading, except I'm not seeing anything on there that would set alarm bells ringing."

Sam peered over her partner's shoulder. "What about something to do with the custody of the child?"

"I can't see anything down here."

"I didn't assume there would be after what Frank told me about the bastard. He also told me several of his customers had used Davis for different building jobs and complained about his work. But like most bullies or those who abuse women, it's a different matter when it comes to dealing with men."

"Yeah, it seems that way. He's got a few parking fines and some minor disturbances of the peace."

"Let's get a couple of people out there to keep an eye on him. Are you up for it?"

"I don't mind, if you're going to be tied up here with the conference and after that, speaking with the parents."

"In other words, you'd prefer to keep out of the way for those two particular chores."

He grinned and leaned in. Lowering his voice, he said, "Shall I take Alex with me?"

"Yes, that's a great idea."

"We'll get on the road. Do you want me to speak to Davis or just keep him under observation for now?"

"If you can find him and think you can handle having a word with him, then do it, but not before you've kept him under observation for half an hour or so, just in case he has his son on site with him. Perhaps, if the opportunity arises, have a sneaky look in the back of his van."

"Gotcha. Alex, fancy a trip out, mate?"

Their Scottish colleague glanced over his shoulder and then looked back at them and pointed to his chest. "Me? Are you sure?"

"Grab your jacket," Bob said impatiently and rose to his feet.

"I'll expect you back in a couple of hours. We'll keep carrying out the necessary checks at this end and be in touch if we need you to come back."

"Roger that," Bob replied. He left the incident room with a bemused Alex rushing to keep up with him.

Sam wandered around the rest of the team. "What else have we got, folks?"

"Nothing new on the footage as yet, boss," Oliver said.

"Stick with it. I know it's a pain in the arse, but it's the only real clue we have that highlights the killers, or one of them at least."

"What do we know about Casey Pardoe? Apart from the obvious, she owns a gym in Workington."

"I researched the name as soon as you called it in earlier and was quite surprised by the amount of newspaper articles I found relating to Casey, not only highlighting her business but also stressing that she was a staunch supporter of women in business. Plus, I found a more recent feature about her backing a new charity in the area that protects and advises women who have escaped abusive relationships," Claire told her.

Sam perched her backside on the desk closest to the sergeant. "Interesting. Maybe that came about because she had the strength to kick Davis out a few years ago. Within this article, does she speak honestly about her own experience with Davis?"

"Give me a second to go through it. Yes, here at the bottom she mentions that women need to gather the strength, followed by needing the support of loved ones, to get them away from abusive partners."

Sam held her hand flat and waved it from side to side. "I wouldn't say she came out and absolutely slated Davis, would you?"

Claire nodded, agreeing with her.

"Let's see what the boys have to say about him when they come back. I don't really want to spend too much time on Davis, only because of what else we're investigating at present." She moved around the room and stopped alongside Suzanna. "You've been sitting here quietly working away for most of the day, don't think for one minute it hasn't gone unnoticed. Are you going to share with us what you've been up to?"

"I will, now that I have finished putting everything together for you, boss."

Sam removed the chair from the spare desk a few feet away and slotted it next to Suzanna's.

"Once I heard there might be a connection between the

two victims, I took it upon myself to research if there had been any other similar deaths in the area in recent months."

"Suicides that could be classed as possible murders?" Sam clarified, her interest piqued.

"Correct. I went back six months and came up with these four women: Jacintha Badam, Rona Clyfford, Yasmin Daccomb and Nancy Hadler."

Sam puffed out her cheeks, dumbfounded by what she was hearing. "I need to have a word with the pathologist, see what he has to say about this, if anything. Maybe there's a connection, maybe not. Can you tell me more about the cases, Suzanna?"

"Starting with Jacintha, she ran her own business, which was a model agency in Workington. She had recently split up with her husband of five years. He was the one who discovered her body when he showed up at her home to collect some of his belongings."

"What was the cause of death?"

"She cut her wrists and was found lying in the bath."

"I can understand that being perceived as a suicide. How about the next one?"

"Rona Clyfford was another successful woman. A few months before her death, she'd suffered a miscarriage after finding out her husband had died in a train crash."

"Jesus, that's a tough set of circumstances for anyone to have to deal with, and what was her COD?"

"Overdose. Her mother hadn't heard from her over the weekend. She'd told her parents she needed space to deal with her grief, and when her mother visited her house to check if she was okay, she discovered Rona lying on the bedroom floor with an empty bottle of pills beside her."

Sam rubbed at her temple. "God, this is making my head hurt. And the next one?"

"Yasmin Daccomb was found in similar circumstances to

Rona Clyfford, a suspected overdose. Her cleaner showed up for duty one day and found her slumped over the kitchen table with a bottle of pills by her side."

Sam struggled to believe that none of the deaths had been investigated more thoroughly, however, she reprimanded herself for thinking that way, given the evidence. "This is unbelievable. What about the final woman?"

"Can I just fill in a blank first?"

"Of course, sorry, I'm jumping ahead. What have you got?"

"Yasmin was also an astute businesswoman; actually, she was an entrepreneur who invested in four businesses deemed to be failures in the area. She turned them around after owning them for six months or under. She was up for the Businesswoman of the Year award last year."

"Amazing, don't tell me someone else pipped her to the title?"

"No, she won it."

"Any kids involved with any of these women?"

"Nothing mentioned in any of the articles. And the final woman is Nancy Hadler. She owned a large restaurant that was down on its knees a few years ago. She spent over half a million renovating it. I did some extra research on this one and unearthed this." Suzanna hit a button, and a dazzling image filled her screen. Dozens of well-known chefs attended the opening to support Nancy.

"God, I don't mind admitting this news is making my stomach churn. Well done, you, for following up on your outstanding hunch."

Suzanna smiled. "All part of the job, boss. Do you want to know how she died?"

"Go for it. Surprise me."

"After the launch party she went straight home and slit her wrists, apparently."

"As you do when you're buzzing after celebrating a success like that. Jesus, what the fuck? Why was all of this not spotted before?" She held her hand up to prevent Suzanna from answering. "It was a rhetorical question. I suppose if we hadn't been involved in the Casey and Gabby cases, we'd be none the wiser, would we? You've really pulled the rabbit out of the bag on this one, Suzanna."

Her cheeks flushed. "I just went along with an idea I had, and it proved to be very profitable, boss. We've done this as a team, there's really no need to single me out for any special praise."

Sam cocked her eyebrow. "Isn't there?"

"I'm with you, boss, she's done an excellent job of finding all that information in less than eight hours," Claire said. She raised her thumb at Suzanna. "Good on ya, Suz."

"Thanks, Claire, it really was nothing."

"Well, without your input we'd still be swimming around a lake, sensing an alligator is about to snap our legs off, so yes, we need to give praise where it's due." Sam patted her on the shoulder and went to walk away but paused. "Something has just come to me. All these women appeared in the local press, right? Only due to their achievements? No wait, that's a silly question, of course it was. What if the killers chose these women because of their instant fame, their accomplishments? Being in the paper was like lighting the touchpaper for the killers. Perhaps it sparked something within them that filled them with anger. Bear with me while I try and figure out what I'm trying to suggest here." Sam closed her eyes and pieced together some of the puzzle in her mind. "We know the killers are connected to someone in prison, who is known to us. What if there's a further connection here? Maybe the killer's mother was successful, perhaps she left the child or children with the husband and set off on her own after she'd achieved success. Perhaps we should go through that list again, Claire, and cross-reference the names with any stories along these lines. Successful women who have walked out on their families, or am I talking a load of rubbish?"

"No, I think your theory has legs. Leave it with me, boss," Claire said and immediately got her head down.

"Suzanna, can you give me the list of names you have created?" Sam peered at the time on her watch. "I've got a spare half an hour. I'd much rather go over something as complex as this in person with the pathologist, but the clock is against me. I'm going to take a punt and give him a call, see if anything comes to mind when I mention the names. Can you check which SIOs were assigned to each case and get a list of family members we can contact if we have to? I know that's asking a lot, but I sense it's important to have all the information to hand now, just in case we need it further down the line."

"Consider it done, boss."

Suzanna jotted down the names and handed the slip of paper to Sam. She went through to her office and rang Des' number. A tech answered his phone and told her he was performing a PM.

"Can you ask him to give me a call at his earliest opportunity? It's important and has something to do with the two murder cases he's dealing with at present."

"I'll leave a note on his desk; he'll pick it up when he's free."

"Damn, thinking about it, our timings might be out of kilter. I have a press conference to attend at four and then I'm meeting up with the parents of the victim who was discovered today. He can try and catch me in between but he needs to be aware of my schedule."

"I'll make sure he understands that, Inspector."

Sam lowered herself into her chair and rubbed the back

of her neck, successfully easing the tension that had gathered since her return. They had so many leads open to them now, she wondered if the team would be able to cope with the amount of work she could foresee ahead of them and soon realised she was doing them all an injustice. She only had to look at each of them individually to see how excited they all were about cracking the case. If anything, she could see they were far more enthusiastic than normal, and she couldn't help wondering if that had anything to do with Rhys being involved. She hoped so. With the spare half an hour she was fortunate to have at her disposal, Sam decided to tackle her mail, appreciating how late in the day it was to be dealing with her daily chore. She was aware that if she didn't, it would never get seen to.

Bob rang her ten minutes later, interrupting her while she was in full flow. "Hi, what's up?"

"We managed to track down Davis. He's currently on site at a house in Schoose. Throwing up an extension that looks as dodgy as hell. I'm tempted to go over there and have a word with the owner of the property, let them know about his dubious reputation."

"Is it really that bad?"

"Yep, Alex is in agreement with me. The damn walls are all wonky, and there's not enough mortar between the joints… anyway, that's not our problem, is it? The owners might be blind for all we know."

"Gosh, I hope not, I'd feel bad if we didn't get involved. For now, we should concentrate on the investigation. It might be worth you having a word with the desk sergeant when you get back, though, get uniform to pop round there, have a quiet word with the property owners."

"I'll do that. In other news, I crept past his vehicle, peered in the back of the van, nothing but tools inside. No sign of the kid."

"Okay, stick with him for half an hour or so and then report back to base. I'll be going downstairs to attend the conference soon, so don't bother ringing me with a further update, not unless anything significant turns up."

"Okey dokey. Good luck with the conference and your meeting with the parents afterwards."

"Thanks, I think I'm going to need it." She ended the call and set aside what was left of her post to make some notes for the conference.

She knew how important it was to have all the facts to hand, just in case any of the crafty journalists tried to trip her up.

TWENTY MINUTES LATER, Sam made her way downstairs to meet up with Jackie Penrose. She ran through the two investigations with Jackie before they tackled the journalists.

"Shit, that's a pretty tough week you're having, Sam. How are you holding up?"

"Okay, sort of. Umm… there's something else I haven't told you."

Jackie inclined her head and frowned. "Go on, we've got a spare five minutes, they're still arriving in there. What's wrong? Is it personal?"

"That's an understatement. At the start of the week, my fella, Rhys, was attacked. It was touch and go whether he survived. Someone knifed him outside his office."

"What? In broad daylight?"

"That's right. In a relatively busy part of town, and yet there were no witnesses to the attack."

"Goodness, and how is he?"

"He's recovering, but I'm livid because the attacker successfully snuck in his room without the staff knowing."

Jackie gasped and gripped Sam's forearm. "No, did he hurt him again while he was in his sickbed?"

"No, at least we don't think so. There's a uniformed officer on duty outside his room now. But the attacker left a note *under* Rhys' body in the bed. I just happened to be the one who found it."

"A note? What did it say? I mean, you don't have to tell me, not if it's personal, Sam."

"It's fine. I thought nothing of it at the time, apart from it scaring the crap out of me, realising that the attacker had gained access to his room. However, since then, my team and I have linked the attack with the two murders we're investigating." Sam fished her phone out of her pocket and showed Jackie the note.

"Bloody hell. So, he specifically targeted Rhys then. Sick fucker."

"Yeah, only because of my involvement. So, you can imagine how that's made me feel."

Jackie handed the phone back to Sam and shook her head. "You can't blame yourself for this Sam, don't you dare, I won't allow you to. Sorry, we're going to have to cut this conversation short and get on with the task in hand. If you want to continue our chat afterwards, I haven't got anything else on."

"Thanks, love. Unfortunately, I have. The second victim's parents are flying back from Portugal; they're landing at two-thirty and coming straight here to see me."

"Ouch. I don't envy you, not in the slightest. You've got a hell of a lot on your plate today. Give me a shout if you need me to dig you out of a hole when we get the conference underway. Okay?"

"Deal. I should be all right; it depends on how brutal the journalists are going to be with me."

"Just give me a nudge under the table with your knee if you need rescuing."

"I'll be sure to do that. Right, let's get this show on the road."

THE CONFERENCE WENT on for longer than either of them anticipated. Sam was right in her perception: the journalists turned out to be brutal with their questions. By the time she and Jackie stepped back into the ante-room, Sam's head felt like it was about to explode.

"Christ, why do they have to go on the attack like that?"

"I feel as though I need to apologise for their behaviour. That was a tough thirty minutes, Sam. I tried to fend off some of the questions, unsuccessfully in certain cases."

"Hey, you did your best, I think we both did, under the circumstances. Christ, I need a gallon of caffeine now before I tackle my next undertaking. Something I'm definitely not looking forward to, especially at the end of the day."

Jackie held out her arms. "I get the impression someone needs a hug."

Sam walked into them. "How did you guess? Thanks, hon. Just what I needed. I'll let you know what sort of feedback, if any, we get from the public on this one."

"Please do. I hope you find the kids soon, they must be frantic, going out of their minds, especially if they saw their mothers being murdered." Jackie shuddered.

"Yep, I definitely wouldn't want to be in their shoes. Hopefully, a member of the public will report that they've seen them. Easy, right?"

"Oh yes, job done and dusted then, eh?" Jackie rolled her eyes.

They both smiled and left the room together but went their separate ways at the top of the stairs.

"Speak soon," Sam shouted after her friend. She pushed open the door to the incident room as someone called her name. She took a step back and looked down the stairs. "What is it, Nick?"

The desk sergeant grinned. "The Pardoes are here to see you."

"Jesus, great timing, not. I was hoping to grab a coffee before I… never mind, I'll be two minutes. Can you show them through to an interview room for me, Nick?"

"Will do. Want me to get you a coffee?"

"You're a saint. Ask them if they need a drink, too."

"Of course."

Sam addressed her team and reported how the conference had gone. "Sorry, I should have asked before, can I have a volunteer to stay behind until tennish, to answer the phones?"

"I'll do it, I've got nothing on this evening," Oliver said.

"Cheers, Oli. Right, I'm off to cross another chore off my to-do list. Casey's parents are downstairs waiting for me. I think I need to pop a couple of ibuprofen first to ward off the headache I have threatening to erupt."

Sam raced through to her office, swallowed two pills with a glug of water from the half-empty bottle sitting on her desk, then she ran a comb through her hair and retraced her steps through the incident room down to the reception area.

Nick glanced up. "I've put them in Interview Room One."

"How are they?" She waved a hand, dismissing her question. "Don't bother answering that." Sam turned and walked down the corridor, her heart pounding, sending shock waves through her nervous system. She entered the room to find three people sitting around the table. Smiling, she introduced herself. "Hello, Mr and Mrs Pardoe, I presume," she said to the older couple. "I'm DI Sam Cobbs. We spoke on the phone earlier."

Mr Pardoe frowned. "Pleased to meet you. I seem to recall seeing your face before, Inspector. Have our paths crossed?"

"A few times in recent years, sir. I'm truly sorry for your loss."

"Can we not beat about the bush here? This is our friend, Gordon Roberts, he's a private investigator."

"Ah, okay." Sam extended her hand to the man in his late thirties. "Pleased to meet you."

"Patrick asked me to meet him and Ivy here, to go over the details of the case with you. I will be working under my own steam during the investigation."

"You will? I must say that it is highly unusual to bring a PI in during the initial stage of an investigation. We have to be given a chance to gather evidence from the scene and allow the pathologist and his team to complete their roles in an investigation."

Gordon opened his mouth to speak, but Sam raised a finger to silence him.

"I rang him about half an hour ago, and he was performing the post-mortem on your daughter."

"Why aren't you in attendance? Isn't it mandatory for the SIO to attend the PM?" Gordon shot back at her.

"No. There was far too much going on here that I needed to oversee."

"Such as?" Gordon queried.

The man's abruptness was already pissing Sam off. "I've not long come out of a press conference which I called earlier today, the second I left Casey's house. Plus, I needed to instruct my team who need constant guidance during an investigation as important as this. I'd also like to bring to your attention the fact this is the second case of this nature my team and I are dealing with this week."

"Oh, well, that's different," Gordon said, having the decency to back down.

Sam sat opposite the three of them and reached for her cup of coffee. "Is this mine?"

Mrs Pardoe nodded. "The desk sergeant kindly brought us each a drink. I'm sorry Gordon bombarded you the second you joined us. We're obviously devastated by what's happened to our daughter, we just didn't know what to do for the best. Patrick contacted Gordon before we left Portugal, to make him aware of what has happened. He had no hesitation in offering his services and agreed to meet us here."

"I've got no aversion to Gordon being here, but I must state from the outset, that he needs to allow us to do our jobs without any interference. My team are exceptionally thorough in every aspect of an investigation. We're going as fast as we can, with the information we've gathered so far."

"I appreciate that. What about Hudson? What are you doing about him?" Gordon demanded, his tone far less abrupt this time.

"As I said, I've just called a press conference. There are also several officers at the house, searching the extensive grounds. We're unsure whether he ran off or whether someone removed him from the house after your daughter was killed. As you're aware, there are no security cameras at the property."

"Please stop stating the obvious. Do you know who did this?" Patrick asked, his voice shaking slightly.

"Not yet. We're working hard to piece together the information we have at our disposal at this time, which I have to tell you, isn't much."

Gordon narrowed his eyes and asked, "What about that bastard of an ex, Kevin Davis? I hope you've pulled him in for questioning?"

"Two of my best officers have got him under surveillance as we speak," she confirmed and prepared herself for the backlash.

"What do you mean by that remark, Inspector?" Patrick asked.

"Exactly what I said, we're watching him."

Both men opened their mouths to interrupt.

"Please, if you'll let me finish. We've put him under surveillance as a precaution, however, I find it hard to consider he's involved in your daughter's death."

"Why? How do you know that?" Patrick asked. "They had a very acrimonious relationship and separation where he threatened our daughter on more than one occasion. I wouldn't put it past him to sink to this level if his aim was to get his son back."

"I can totally understand where you're coming from and, I assure you, I would be assuming the same, if it wasn't for the other murder we're investigating."

"Sorry, you've lost me," Mrs Pardoe said. "Can someone explain what she's on about?"

"I can't," Patrick said. He gripped his wife's hand. "Care to explain, Inspector?"

Sam nodded. "We're finding it very difficult to overlook the similarities we've uncovered between the two murders."

The three people all seemed confused by her explanation.

"What are you saying? That the two murders were committed by a serial killer?" Gordon finally asked.

"Possibly. My team are busy upstairs going through dozens of previous cases, searching for clues. The stumbling block in both crimes is that both properties were situated out in the middle of nowhere, without any form of security in place. You're all aware of what a significant part CCTV footage plays in solving crimes these days."

Mr and Mrs Pardoe and Gordon stared at Sam. Causing her to feel uncomfortable.

"We're also up against the fact there were no witnesses at either location. Again, without having any key witnesses to call upon, it makes our job that much harder."

Mrs Pardoe started to cry. "Then how are you going to find the person who is responsible for taking our daughter from us?"

"We're hoping the press conference will produce the leads that will prove to be beneficial to both investigations. What I need to ask is if Casey had confided in either of you, if something had been troubling her lately. I'm aware that she was in the process of opening a second gym in the area. Had she come across any problems with that project?"

Both parents shook their heads.

"No, quite the opposite, in fact," Mr Pardoe said. "Up until the minute we took off for our holiday, Casey told us all her plans were falling into place perfectly. You can imagine how shocked we were when you called us this morning and broke this disturbing news to us. We've discussed it non-stop during the trip back, and the only problematic person who came to mind was Kevin Davis. It brought back all the vile outbursts we witnessed during their turbulent relationship." His head bowed, and he stared at his hand linked with his wife's.

"You know he abused her, don't you?" his wife said.

"Yes, a member of my team has carried out extensive research regarding your daughter and discovered several articles in which she briefly mentioned escaping an abusive relationship. I also read that she was heavily involved in a charity which assists vulnerable women."

"Yes, she overcame her own issues of mistrust and hatred for her ex, to give strength to other women to help them escape the clutches of the vile men they are living with," Mrs Pardoe said with immense pride in her voice.

"Did she ever say she didn't feel safe at the house?"

"No, not that I can recall," Mr Pardoe replied. "Asking all these inane questions isn't going to help capture her killer. You and your team should be out there, not only searching for our grandson but also looking high and low for our daughter's murderer."

"As I'm sure you'll appreciate, we need to carry out the necessary groundwork before we can start banging on people's doors to interview them. What about at the gym? Had she fallen out with anyone at work, possibly due to the stressful environment?"

"No, never. Her team have always been very supportive. They're all female, as are most of her clients, I believe," Mrs Pardoe added before blowing her nose on a tissue. "Why don't we go home, Patrick? Let the inspector get on with her job. Will you work with Gordon, Inspector?"

"I'm sorry, that's not how the Force works. We have certain procedures to follow. If we don't, then I'm sure you know what the consequences of any slip-ups would mean once they get to court."

Mr and Mrs Pardoe nodded, but Gordon stared at Sam, putting her on edge.

"You wouldn't be warning me off, would you, Inspector?"

"Not at all. I'm merely stating facts. I can't prevent you from, shall we say, probing the crime. Providing you don't interfere with our investigation and become a hindrance. I believe we're all hoping to achieve the same outcome, after all."

"I'll be concentrating on Davis, he's the boy's father, therefore, in my mind he should be at the top of your list for a suspect."

"Not wishing to repeat myself, but the fact that we have an ongoing investigation…"

"Yes, yes, you made it quite clear why you're willing to let him off being brought in for questioning," Gordon snapped. "I'm inclined to think that's a major faux pas on your part."

"You're entitled to your opinion, as am I. Now, if you'll excuse me, I really should get back to the incident room."

Mr Pardoe stood. "Is that it? We travelled all the way back from Portugal to have a ten-minute conversation with you?"

"I'm sorry. The longer I spend going over the case with the family, the less time I can contribute to finding the killer. I'll show you back to reception."

A strange sensation swept through her as she walked ahead of the three visitors; it felt like they were examining her every move under a microscope.

When she reached the reception, she rolled her eyes at Nick then turned to shake her visitors' hands. "Again, I'm truly sorry for your loss, Mr and Mrs Pardoe. I'll be in touch as soon as I have any significant news for you." She gave them one of her cards.

Gordon put his hand in his pocket and did exactly the same. "I'll give you one of mine, too. Ring me if you need an extra body to help out during the investigation."

Sam took the card and smiled. "I'm sure that won't be necessary, but I'll keep it safe, just in case." Her mobile rang, giving her the excuse to get away. "I need to answer this. I'll be in touch. Take care."

She heard their mumbled responses before the security door closed behind her. She expelled a relieved breath and answered the phone. "Bob, how are things going over there?"

"I was checking with you first before we leave. There's really nothing to see here. We've observed him getting on with his day and ordering his men around as if he hasn't got a care in the world. He's not once looked over his shoulder, if you get my drift?"

"I do. As suspected, I don't think he can be involved because of what happened to Gabby. Come back to the station, we'll go over what the team have come up with at the end and then go home."

"Sounds good to me. How did the conference go?"

"It went on longer than Jackie and I anticipated it would. Hopefully, that'll be to our advantage. We won't know that for sure until the appeal is aired later. Oliver has volunteered to stay behind this evening to answer any calls that might come in. And don't ask how it went with the parents."

Bob laughed. "In that case, I won't. We'll head back then. See you soon."

"You will."

Sam trudged her way back up the stairs on wobbly legs. The last half an hour with Casey's parents had sapped what little strength she had left this late in the day.

"How did it go?" Claire said, immediately jumping out of her seat to make Sam a coffee.

"Let's just say it went. The parents weren't alone, they had a PI with them. I'm hoping the warning I gave him will be enough for him to think twice before he gets under our feet but, somehow, I doubt it."

Claire delivered her coffee. "Wow, that's a new one. What are they hoping to achieve, apart from the obvious?"

"I think they just wanted to enforce upon me the fact that they're prepared to do what's necessary to get their grandson back. Which is all well and good, except that's our main aim as well. Thanks for the drink, Claire. I need to have five minutes in my office to process what's taken place today. Bob and Alex are on their way back."

"Okay, boss. Give us a shout if you need anything. We're still cross-referencing all the names et cetera."

"I was thinking about that before I attended the conference. It might be an idea to get in touch with the families of the victims, see if any of them are willing to have a word with us."

Claire pulled a face. "Do you think? Some of the cases span back six months or slightly more."

"I hear you. Let's do it, for my peace of mind then. We need to find out if any of the families had an inkling the victims had hinted about committing suicide."

"Leave it with me, I'll see what I can find out."

Sam completed the rest of the paperwork she'd set aside earlier on and drank her coffee over the next fifteen minutes, until a knock on the door interrupted her.

Bob poked his head into the room. "Hi, that's us back. Shall I grab a coffee and join you?"

"You might as well."

Two minutes later, he entered the room with two mugs of coffee.

"Christ, it's a good job I haven't got a weak bladder, I'd probably spend more time in the loo than on the investigation."

He grinned, but then his expression turned serious once more. "You seem down, are you?"

"I wouldn't say that, maybe feeling my age at the end of a long, stressful day."

"I suppose it doesn't help with Rhys being in hospital, either."

"You've hit the nail on the head there, partner. I'm trying to keep that in the background but, I'm struggling to do that, only because of his suspected involvement in the case."

"I can understand that. Where do we go from here?"

"We cross our fingers and hope the general public can help us out tonight. The girls have come up with a possible list of four extra victims."

"What? Why only possible?"

"All four deaths were classed as suicides at the time due to the CODs."

His eyes narrowed. "What are you saying? You think the killers were perfecting their skills on these individuals?"

Sam nodded. "Yep, although the crimes were different, in that the victims didn't have any children. Leading me to wonder what changed along the way. There's also the question as to why the deaths weren't investigated properly at the time, either. I've got to talk to Des about that, although I don't want it to come across as accusatory when I speak with him."

"Jesus, are you sure about this? It wouldn't be like him to miss something as obvious, would it?"

Sam shrugged and tapped the pen she was holding on the desk. "I can't see it happening myself, but then the whole department has been under immense pressure lately. Don't forget his assistant resigned around about that time, too."

Bob sipped at his drink. "I'd forgotten that. Definitely something to consider. Silly question coming up, how did it go with the parents?"

She told him about the PI showing up and throwing his weight around during the meeting and then said wearily, "Right, I'm calling it a day. It's been full on today and it's not over yet. I still have to stop off at the hospital on the way home."

"You shoot off, I can handle things here."

"Are you sure?"

"This is a one-time-only offer."

Sam smiled and slipped on her jacket. "In that case, I'll take you up on your offer. Is it wrong of me to hope that Rhys is asleep when I get there? I could do with getting an early night."

"Must be exhausting for you showing willingness every

day, plus you're going to need to squeeze in walking the dogs and fixing yourself something to eat as well."

"Don't remind me. Yep, I'd say I've got a pretty busy evening ahead of me."

"All the more reason for you to head off now. There's nothing else you can do here, it's all down to what comes in from the public, and that's not likely to happen until later this evening."

"You're right. I'll see you bright and early in the morning. Hopefully, we'll have dozens of calls vying for our attention first thing."

"I doubt it, but you never know. We might get the shock of our lives."

CHAPTER 9

"They're playing up again," Adam complained.

Ian laughed. "It's what kids do. You were the same at their age."

"I wasn't. I dispute that, I was always good for you and Mum, from what I can remember."

"That's called having a selective memory. You were a whiny kid. I had to whack your backside a few times, I can tell you, especially in the early days. I bet the problem with these kids is they've had their own way for too long. Not had to deal with any form of discipline because the mothers were too wrapped up in their work to even bother with them."

"Umm… I think you'll find the rules have changed… you're no longer allowed to give your kids a good hiding."

"And that's where society is failing," Ian grumbled. "Anyway, we can't hang around here, arguing the toss about the right and wrong ways to bring up kids, we've got another job to do tonight. I need to make a few notes first. Can I leave you to feed the evil ones?"

"Do you think they're getting fed up with beans on toast yet?"

"Tough shit if they are. It's all we've got, so they either eat it or starve, it's as simple as that."

"When do you want to head off?"

"Around eight-thirty. So, you've got two hours to feed and water them and shove them back in the cellar."

"It should be a doddle."

Adam left the lounge, and Ian went over the plans he'd found online for their next victim's house.

We're going to need to be a bit more careful this time around, her home is quite close to a couple of others, not like the previous ones.

Within the hour, he had what he felt was an appropriate plan in place. Adam had fed the kids, not that they'd eaten much, and put them in the temporary cell they had made in the cellar.

They left their property at five minutes to eight. The victim's home was over half an hour's drive away.

Ian felt anxious throughout the journey. "Maybe we should reconsider the time, leave it until a bit later."

"Why?"

"Look at how light it is. I hadn't taken that into consideration when I came up with this plan."

"Do you want to stop off somewhere first?" Adam suggested. "I could do with a pint."

"Good shout. There's a pub en route. When we stop off, don't do anything that will bring attention to yourself."

"Goes without saying."

Ian drew into the car park, which was almost full, and they entered the Brown Cow pub. He ordered a couple of pints of beer, and they found a table in the corner, close to the unlit inglenook fireplace. Being strangers to the area, they automatically stood out in the crowd. Something about the way the locals were staring at him gave Ian the jitters.

He leaned in and ordered, "Sup up, we're out of here."

"Christ, give me a chance, Dad."

Five minutes later, with their drinks finished, they hit the road again.

"Shit! That wasn't the experience we needed, especially tonight," Ian grumbled.

"Yeah, the beer was shit, too."

They continued the rest of the journey in silence.

Ian was relieved to see the old farmhouse was tucked back a little from the other properties in the small village. He found the location and the position of the property still wasn't ideal, but then, they'd been forced to endure far worse problems over the years. "Are you ready for this?"

"What? You can't stop here, just outside the property?"

"Don't be such an idiot. I'm not, I'm going to tuck the van behind this wall. I'm thinking we're going to need to have the van close to hand this evening. It pays to be prepared."

Adam shrugged. "Whatever. That's your call."

"It is. Let's not hang around out here, we need to get the job done. I want to be in and out within half an hour this time."

"Any particular reason?"

Ian tutted. "Because it's still light."

"Whatever."

Ian thumped his son in the arm. "Get the bag, hurry." He anxiously glanced up and down the road, unsure whether they were doing the right thing or not, approaching the house at this time of night. The thought occurred to him that they to back out but, in the end, his stubbornness prompted him to continue. He flinched at the sound of the van door being slammed shut. "What the fuck are you doing?"

"Sorry," Adam apologised. "I clipped it with the bag, and the door was out of reach before I had a chance to stop it."

Ian scanned the area. Luckily, there was no movement, from what he could tell, in any of the nearby houses. "It doesn't matter, I think we got away with it this time. Be careful from now on."

"It was an accident, they happen, you know," Adam replied cheekily.

"Believe me, I should know. Your mother said the same when she told me she was pregnant with you." The shock on his son's face made him snigger. "Let's get in there, get this job done."

Ian led the way on to the property, ensuring they kept to the edge of the boundaries; he was aware that the lounge faced the entrance. "We'll get closer to the house around the side, we're less likely to be seen there." He summoned up the image for the layout of the property and established that the woman's study would be within ten feet of where they were now. "We'll go round the back, see if the door is open."

They crept across the lawn, hiding behind the various fruit trees masking them from the road, until they made it to the rear of the house.

Ian was shocked to see the woman sitting on the patio, speaking to someone on the phone. She laughed now and again and sipped at her glass of wine.

"Okay, Shirley. I'm going in now; I'd better check on Damien. Glad everything is going well, I can't wait to see you walking down the aisle in a couple of weeks… Not long to wait now… Love you." She ended the call and tipped her head back, catching the last of the sun's rays as it dipped down behind the property in the distance. After several minutes she stood, tidied up the furniture and took her glass inside the house. Ian gestured for Adam to quickly move towards the end of the house.

He caught the sound of the door being locked and grunted. "Shit, now we're going to have to wait until she's away from the kitchen. If there's no cat flap, we're going to need to break in." He opened the bag Adam had put on the ground beside him and rummaged around for the pin hammer and a cloth that would help to deaden the noise.

They waited another couple of moments before Ian made his move. He peered through the small kitchen window; there was no sign of the woman in the room. They approached the back door. There was no cat flap either. That left them little option but to break a pane in the back door. But first, Ian checked if it was open. He wrapped the cloth around the hammer and struck the window with a tap in the corner. The glass smashed, and Ian shoved his gloved hand through it to turn the key. He knew how important it was to get in the house quickly, in case the noise had alerted the woman. "Stick behind me, avoid stepping on the glass when we get inside."

"I'm not stupid," Adam whispered back.

They entered the house and closed the door behind them. Despite Adam assuring his father that he would steer clear of the glass, he didn't, and it crunched under his feet.

"Is anyone there?" the woman said from the hallway.

Ian pointed to the right; there was a utility room off the kitchen. They dived in there, making it in the nick of time. From their hiding place, Ian could see the woman had come prepared; she had a poker raised in her right hand.

"I know you're in here. I'm warning you now, if you don't come out by the time I get to three, I'm calling the police, they can bloody deal with you."

It was then Ian noticed the small mobile she was holding in her other hand. He decided to call the woman's bluff and broke cover. Adam grabbed his jacket.

"Don't do it, stay here," his son hissed.

"I'm in charge, I'll do what I want."

The woman opened her mouth, as if about to scream.

He held up his hand. "Do that and we'll kill your son. Drop the weapon."

The woman hesitated but only for a moment, then she came at Ian with the poker aimed at his midriff. He flicked his arm as she got close. She toppled to the side and then rammed into his chest with a thud, sending them both off balance.

"Get the rope, tie her up, son."

Adam dipped his hand into the bag and removed a length of rope. He tussled with it, trying to find the end while his father grappled with the woman.

Ian took advantage of the clear shot and punched the woman in the face, knocking her out cold. She slid to the floor. "Jesus, we need to get her secured quickly, she's feistier than the others, which will prove to be her downfall come the end."

Between them they bound the woman and carried her from the kitchen into the lounge. The floorboards creaked upstairs, alerting them to the fact that the boy was still awake up there.

"Go get the kid. We're going to have to alter our plans."

Adam ran up the stairs. A door slammed overhead, and Damien's screams filled the room above. Adam shouted to let him in but ended up breaking the door down. The kid's screams got worse as Adam carried him along the hallway and down the stairs to join Ian and the boy's mother in the lounge.

"Mummy… what have you done to her?" The kid sobbed and fought to get to his mother.

"Keep hold of him. We'll have to tie him to the chair."

"No… I won't let you." Damien kicked out at Adam and bit his arm.

Adam let the kid go to check his wound, but Ian stood in the child's path, preventing him from leaving the room. He whipped the boy up into the air, holding him at arm's length.

"Stop squirming or I'm going to hurt your mummy."

The child instantly stopped wriggling. "Who are you?"

"Wouldn't you like to know? Now I'm going to put you in this chair, and you're going to allow me to tie you to it, or, well, you know what the consequences are going to be."

The teary-eyed boy nodded his understanding, his gaze locked on his mother. "Mummy?" he called, eager to gain her attention.

Between them, Ian and Adam successfully tied both the mother and child to two dining chairs. Within seconds, the woman woke up.

Her head slumped to the right. "What... what do you want?"

"You, Odell," Ian said and grinned.

She flinched and shook her head to clear it. "Do I know you?"

"No, but I know all about you and little Damien here."

Her gaze swept the room and landed on her son. "Don't hurt us, I'm begging you not to hurt my son. He's only five."

"I know how old he is."

"How do you know that? I repeat, what do you want with us?"

Ian's smile broadened. "We're going to have some fun with you."

Odell's eyes widened. "What are you talking about?" She shook her head as the realisation dawned. "Don't do this, not in front of Damien. If it's money you want, I can give you some, but it's going to take me a few hours to get hold of a large sum."

"It's not. Enough of this, I'm bored already." Ian withdrew a tub of tablets from the bag and tipped some into his hand. "Swallow them."

Odell clamped her mouth shut and shook her head.

Ian gestured for his son to join him. "Force her mouth open."

Odell swished her head from side to side, determined not to allow them access to her mouth.

"You're foolish if you think that's going to stop me. Open your mouth or I'll shove them down Damien's throat. The choice is yours."

Tears erupted and landed on her flushed cheeks. "Why? What is wrong with you? Why are you doing this to us? I can't do it... I refuse to do it."

"That's up to you." Ian walked over to her son, grabbed him by the hair and yanked his head back. When the child screamed out in pain, Ian dropped one of the pills into his mouth.

"No... no... Damien, spit it out, love, don't swallow it."

But her son didn't get the chance to spit it out, not with his head still tipped back. He sobbed. Foam mixed with spittle seeped from the corners of his mouth. Ian gripped the boy's chin and forced his mouth open. Damien squealed and swallowed the tablet.

Ian and Adam laughed, and Damien glanced at his mother and cried. "I'm sorry, Mummy, I didn't mean to do it. He hurt me... so, so much."

"It's all right, my darling. Don't worry. Stay strong, angel, and everything will be okay, I promise you."

"I don't think you're in a position to make empty promises, do you?"

"But... what else can I do to make you see sense, to leave us alone?"

"Nothing. Now are you going to take the pills or not? My patience is being tested more and more by your refusal."

"But why?" She choked on the sobs caught in her throat.

"Take them and we'll get out of your hair."

"I won't. Why should I kill myself just because you tell me to?"

Ian ground his teeth and sneered, "You're running the risk of us killing you both, is that what you want?"

"No, I've lived a full life, my son's is just beginning. What am I saying? I don't know any more. I don't understand what this is all about. Why do you want me to kill myself?" She shuddered.

"I'm not here to debate the topic with you. I've told you what will happen if you don't take the tablets. So, what's it to be?"

"Forgive me, but I can't…"

He took two paces towards her son, and she screamed.

"Okay, okay, I'll do it. I'm sorry, Damien. Mummy loves you with all her heart. I want you to remember that for the rest of your life."

"Mummy, no. Don't say that. I don't understand. We love each other… why? I don't… want… to lose you. You're all I've got."

Ian placed his hand on Damien's shoulder and leaned down to speak with him. "Don't worry, son, you're going to be well looked after. You're going to come and live with us. We're going to train you, just like the other little boys we have staying with us at the house."

"To do what?" Odell screeched.

Ian faced her and smiled. "To be serial killers. I'm ensuring the next generation succeeds where our predecessors failed."

Odell gasped. "No, this can't be true, you can't be serious. What type of person are you, to want to corrupt innocent children?"

"I've just told you. I'm a serial killer, proud to be one, and yes, I'm lacking in morals, aren't we all nowadays?" He tipped his head back and laughed.

"But what you're thinking of doing… is disgusting."

"Correction, not thinking of doing, I am doing it. Say hello to my first protégé." He gestured to Adam.

Odell shook her head several times, finally rendered speechless.

"Now, this is the final chance to do the right thing. Let's face it, it's no skin off my nose if your son dies with you, there will be plenty of other opportunities out there for us to gather more recruits."

"But why Damien? Have you specifically targeted him over me?"

Ian winked and tapped his nose. "And there we have it, the penny has dropped, finally. I don't give women much credit or I haven't done since his mother walked out on us to fulfil her ambitions to be an entrepreneur, but your type must have something about you to raise a child and work the hours you do to maintain your exceptional businesses. Which means, your kids will have outstanding genes."

"Jesus, I can't believe what I'm hearing. Is this what you being in my house is all about? I saw a copper on the news tonight, pleading for information about two young boys who had been kidnapped and whose mothers had been killed. Was that you?"

Ian breathed on his fingernails and then polished them on his chest. "Guilty as charged. Hey, it's not like you or the others we've killed care about your kids, is it?"

"Mummy, what's he going to do with us?" Damien asked, his voice as squeaky as that of a mouse.

"Don't worry, sweetheart, these men aren't going to hurt you, they wouldn't dare."

"Don't test me, lady. Don't you dare do that. Now effing take the pills and get this over with."

He removed a bottle of brandy from his bag. "I brought this along, it's only cheap shit, it's not exactly Courvoisier, my pockets ain't that deep."

"I hate brandy."

"Tough." He approached her again with a dozen or so pills in his hand. "Last chance, and I mean it. We've been here far too long as it is."

Odell took one last look at her son and whispered, "Forgive me, Damien."

"No, Mummy, don't!" Damien screamed.

"Put some tape over the kid's mouth. I'm fed up of messing about. Now swallow them."

Odell complied, opened her mouth, then closed her eyes and, with large tears streaming down her cheeks, gulped down the tablets along with the brandy on offer. She coughed and spluttered, but that came after she had swallowed down the contents of her mouth.

"Success at last. Right, they should kick in soon, but just to be sure, here's another handful."

With her gaze fixed on her son, Odell swallowed the next batch of pills without any further defiance. Her eyelids began to droop. It proved to be an impossible task to prevent her eyes closing a final time, and she whispered, "I love you, Damien. Get away from them when you can."

The boy squirmed in his seat and tried to shout a response to his dying mother, but his words were silenced by the tape. He stared at his mother, unable to turn away.

"Okay, I've had a thought," Ian announced. "I'm going to do something different with this one."

Adam took a step towards his father and asked, "What's that?"

"We're going to take her with us and dump her body on the way. That'll get the cops thinking. Watching that appeal going out tonight, I got the impression that bitch copper knows what our plans are. Let's shake it up a bit, shall we?"

Adam smiled and rubbed his hands together. "That's the

best thing you've said all day, Dad. Do you want me to untie them now?"

"Yeah, take the boy out to the van, secure him in the back, then drive up to the front door."

"What? Are you sure? What if the neighbours see us?"

Ian pointed to his face. "Do I look bothered?" Then he laughed and didn't stop until Adam left the house with the boy. He crouched beside Odell. "All this could have been avoided, if only you hadn't let that mouth run away from you." He shook her shoulder. "I want you to stay awake now, to see what else we have planned for you." He untied her hands and lifted her over his shoulder. It was a huge effort, doing it on his own. Then he carried her through the house and out of the front door, which he left open on purpose.

Adam had the back of the van open, ready for him to dump Odell's body. They secured her with a rope tightened around her waist, opposite her frantic son.

"Let them have the last ten minutes of her life together."

Ian took the keys from his son, and they both hopped in the front. Ian sped out of the drive, not caring if he drew attention to them leaving or not. He had the ideal spot in mind. They had passed it on the way there.

He drove to the location. The river was quite low at the moment, but it was still flowing fast enough for what he intended. It was getting dark now, which helped ease the anxiety he would have normally had, regarding dumping the body out in the open. "Come on, we need to get a shift on."

Adam ran to the back and pulled the doors open. Odell was still conscious which added to Ian's excitement.

"Still with us, Odell, that's great. I do like it when a plan comes together."

Between them, they removed her body from the van and walked five feet to the water's edge. She wriggled, but the movement was minimal, not enough to cause them any inconvenience. They left her hands tied. Adam had slapped some tape over her mouth when he'd put her in the back of the van.

"I think we'll leave her here, suspended in the water. The current will take her soon enough, but being stuck on the bank, out here in the dark, will add to her torture."

"You have a wicked streak running through you, Dad, and I love it. How far in shall we put her."

"Dangle her legs in it. Let the water reach mid-thigh. That should do the trick."

They positioned Odell on the riverbank. She stared up at them and shook her head but said nothing, not that they would have heard her anyway.

Ian slapped Adam in the chest. "Right, let's get the boy back to the farm."

CHAPTER 10

*S*am felt bone-tired the following morning. She'd had to force herself to get out of bed to take the dogs for a walk at six-thirty. Guilt was attacking her from all angles at the moment, and it was hard for her to fend off. She had visited Rhys the previous evening, but when she arrived, he was sound asleep. She hadn't bothered sitting at his bedside for hours on end, no, she'd pecked him on the cheek and left him right away, knowing that she had other responsibilities that needed dealing with elsewhere. Vernon had texted her to tell her that he'd taken Sonny and Casper for a couple of long walks during the day and delivered them back to Doreen who was thrilled to be looking after both the dogs.

She was blessed to have genuinely kind people around her in her hour of need. The same proposal was on the cards for the dogs today, however, she was determined to play her part in the scheme, hence getting up half an hour earlier than normal.

Once they returned from their walk and Sam had fed the dogs, she jumped in the shower and dried her hair. Then she dropped the dogs off at Doreen's. Her neighbour was thrilled to see them all standing at her front door.

"I'm in my element, Sam. They're wonderful and keep me on the go all day with their exuberance, but I wouldn't have it any other way. Vernon mentioned he'd call for them at lunchtime, so don't you go worrying about them."

"I won't. I know they're in safe hands. I can't thank you enough for taking care of them for me, Doreen, I know it's a lot to ask of you."

"Nonsense. It was my suggestion. Now leave them with me and go and find those nasty people who have taken those children and killed their mothers."

"So, you saw the appeal go out last night? It's been an horrendous week, furthermore, not many people know this, we believe there might be a connection between the two investigations and the attack on Rhys."

Doreen gasped and slapped her hands on either side of her face. "Goodness me, how awful. Your emotions must be all over the place, Sam."

"I'm doing my best to keep them in check, not sure I've succeeded thus far." She gave her neighbour a hug and thanked her again. "I really do appreciate all you do for us."

"I know you do, and that's all that matters. Now, shoo… you have criminals to capture."

"I'll see you later. Don't stand for any bad behaviour from these two, either." She handed Doreen the two leashes and waited until the front door was closed before she turned to walk towards the car. When she peered over her shoulder, the three of them were at the lounge window, but only Doreen waved her off.

Bob pulled into his space alongside hers, and they strolled towards the station together.

"You look tired, but I'm not surprised."

"I'm fine. I can cope, providing I get a good night's sleep. How are things at home?"

"Same as always. Nothing ever changes, not really. And Rhys, how was he last night?"

"Asleep when I got there. I felt guilty going home early and not sitting with him."

"You shouldn't. It's just as important for you to get your rest when you can."

"I'm doing better than anticipated, thanks to Vernon and Doreen. I don't think the dogs have suffered at all this week. I hope not, anyway."

"They can be pretty resilient. Did Oliver call you last night before he finished?"

"Yes, the phones had only rung a couple of times. He sounded despondent. I told him to come in at midday, so we're going to be a body light this morning."

"I'm sure we'll cope. Want me to oversee the proceedings this morning, while you get on with your paperwork?"

She chuckled. "Sounds like you have my day all planned out for me."

"I... er... no, I wasn't..."

She slapped his arm. "I'm messing with you. First, let's assess what's come in overnight and go from there, eh?"

"Agreed. Fingers crossed something comes our way soon. I'm not sure what else we can do if it doesn't."

"You've got that right."

Bob opened the front door for Sam, and she entered the reception area to find Nick frantically throwing sheets of paper in the air.

"Hey, what's going on?"

"I've just come on duty, don't ask, my car wouldn't start this morning and, well... sorry, I was about to give you a call."

"Sounds ominous. What's up, Nick?"

"It might be nothing, but I'm inclined to believe it has something to do with the investigations you're dealing with at present."

Sam took a few steps closer to the desk. "Go on."

"We received a report, at around ten-thirty last night, that a woman had been found lying on a riverbank. She was unconscious when the ambulance arrived. They managed to wake her up, but what she told them didn't make sense. Turns out she was forced to take tablets with brandy."

"What? Where was this?"

He handed her a slip of paper with the location. "She was found by a man walking his dog down by the river. He's already given us a statement; there was no one else in the area, and a vehicle didn't pass him either."

"Bugger! Thanks, Nick. Can you tell my team we're on the way to the hospital to have a word with the victim? What about the appeal? Any calls come in overnight, or aren't you up to date on that yet?"

"I've got a few. I'll nip them upstairs now and inform your team at the same time."

"That would be great." Sam raced back to the car with Bob just behind her.

"Are you up to driving, or do you want to pass your keys over to me?" Bob asked.

"I'm fine. Stop fussing. This could be the break we've been waiting for."

AT THE HOSPITAL, the woman turned out to be on the floor above Rhys. If they had time, Sam made a mental note to check in with him before they left.

Odell Ebery was resting when they entered the room. A

nurse was checking her vital signs and writing them on the chart.

Sam showed her ID. "We're desperate to speak with her, can you tell us what happened?"

"She hasn't said much really. I think she's too traumatised. Her body is forcing her to rest, to combat the shock."

"I completely understand but…"

"Who… are you?" Odell woke up and asked.

Sam approached the bed and introduced herself, at the same time she flashed her ID. "Are you up to speaking with us, Odell?"

"Yes. I need you to find my son. Two men have taken him."

"Can you give us a description of the men?"

"I think they're father and son. My head is a little muzzy… they forced sleeping tablets or something like that down my throat, along with a glug or two of brandy. I refused to take them for so long, but they threatened to give them to my son instead." She broke down.

Sam glanced up at the nurse.

"She should rest. This is too much for her to cope with at this time," the nurse insisted.

"No, don't send them away. I need to speak with them, I have important information I want to share. You have to get my son back."

"We're going to do our best. Can you run through what happened?" Sam asked the distraught woman.

"I'd put Damien to bed, he's five. I went downstairs, tidied up the kitchen, then my friend rang me. I poured a glass of wine and sat in the garden while I chatted with her for ten minutes or so. Then I went back inside and locked the door behind me. I was sorting something out in my study, and I thought I heard something break in the kitchen. I had the feeling someone was trying to break into my house. In hindsight, I should have rung the police instead of thinking I could handle it myself. I called out, told the intruders to show themselves or I'd call the police." She closed her eyes and shook her head. "Why on earth didn't I make the call?"

"Please, stop castigating yourself. I'm sure I would have done the same in your shoes," Sam assured her.

"I doubt it. Two men came out of the utility room. One of them, the older man, knocked me out. I had a poker in my hand and tried to use it on him; maybe that was the wrong move on my part. I woke up to find my son sitting in a chair close to me. He was in tears, screaming, crying out for me to help him, but I couldn't because they had tied me to the chair. I regret arguing with the older man. He forced my son to swallow one of the tablets because I refused to take them. I didn't know what to do for the best. He gave me little option other than to swallow them in the end. My poor Damien, for him to have witnessed the torture and torment the men put me through must have been terrifying for him."

"I'm sorry you had to go through that. Can you tell us anything else? Did the men say why they wanted to kidnap your son?"

Tears emerged and dripped onto her cheek. "Yes, I couldn't believe my ears when the older man told me he was kidnapping the children with the intention of turning them into future serial killers. I didn't know what to do or say to that revelation. To know they were about to kill me, abduct my son and... I can't think about it, I refuse to give the idea a second thought. Please, you have to find him, find them. I saw the news bulletin last night, the other successful women who have had their sons taken this week. There has to be a connection, doesn't there?"

"Can I ask what you do for a living?"

"I'm an exclusive fashion designer. My clientele is rich and famous, some are even royalty. My studio is in London, but I prefer to live and work up here. I travel to London once a month. I trust my second-in-command to deal with the day-to-day running of the studio. He's in contact with me daily. Between us, we make it work. I was brought up around here. I wanted my son to benefit from the fresh air and peaceful way of life, living in the country. And look where that has got me. I'm devastated beyond words knowing that I might never see my little man again."

"Please, try to remain positive. I know you're tired, but what can you tell us about the two men?"

"I think they're father and son, only because one of them called the other Dad. His name was Adam."

Bob withdrew his notebook and scribbled down the details.

Thank God we've got a lead to go on, at last. But we're going to need far more than just his name.

"Is there any chance you can give us a description of the two men? If we brought a police sketch artist in, perhaps?"

"Yes, I think that would be a good idea. Do it soon, while their images are fresh in my mind."

"I'll get that arranged ASAP. What type of vehicle did they have?"

"They drove me to the location in a dark van, either black or navy blue. The light was fading fast at the time, and I wasn't really thinking straight due to the effects of the tablets kicking in."

Possibly the van we've been searching for. "Did you happen to overhear where they were intending to take your son?"

"Hang on, yes, they said something about getting back to the farm… I think. Please, that's all I know. Is it enough for you to work with?"

"We're going to do all we can to reunite you with your son. I'll leave my card on the table here. If you think of anything else, please ring me."

"Yes, I'll do that." She held up her hand, and Sam squeezed it. "Please, find my son," she pleaded, fresh tears welling up.

Sam smiled. "We will, I promise. Get some rest. We'll arrange for the sketch artist to come and see you today. Take care."

"Thank you." Odell closed her eyes, clearly exhausted.

Sam and Bob raced back to the station. As soon as she entered the incident room, she shouted good morning and made her way over to Claire.

"That list of inmates I've put away over the years, have you got it?"

"It's here, along with any personal details I could find about their family members." Claire handed her a sheet of paper, and Sam ran her finger down the list. "We've got a couple of possibilities here. Two convicts with sons. Let's see what we can find out about them."

IT DIDN'T TAKE Claire long to research the relevant facts. By the time Oliver joined them at midday, Sam's gut instinct was on full alert. She gathered the team together to go over the information each of them had sourced.

"One of the convicts, Joel Fisher, had a son. He died a couple of years ago in an accident abroad," Claire said.

"So, that leaves us with Denis Walcott. What do we know about him? Is he from this area?" Sam asked.

"He is, born and bred here. His father was… shit," Claire's gaze frantically met Sam's. "He's a local farmer."

Sam shot across the room. "Where? Is he still alive? What about the name Adam?"

"Holy crap, I think we've got them. Adam is Denis Walcott's grandson; his father is Ian Walcott. The grandfather died last year. His property is out in Little Clifton."

"Was it sold? Or passed down to relatives in his will?"

"I can check. Give me fifteen minutes," Claire replied and feverishly tapped at her keyboard.

"I think we should get out there," Bob suggested excitedly.

"I'm inclined to agree with you. We're going to need backup, but I can sort that out with Nick on our way out. Claire, can you get back to me with that information while we're en route?"

"Of course."

"Oliver, Liam, Alex, you set off in one car. Suzanna, do you fancy coming with us? I'm going to need help with the kids, if we find them, and no, that's not a sexist comment."

"I don't mind, boss. I've had a bit of experience, looking after my sister's two kids. They're six and four."

"That's perfect. Let's get out there."

ON THEIR WAY through the reception area, they ran into four uniformed officers who were reporting for duty. Nick immediately assigned them to Sam as backup. She gave them a quick lowdown on what she expected from them when they got to the farm. Sam and Oliver also signed out a couple of Tasers before they got on the road.

"It's five minutes away now," Bob said.

Sam put her foot down. They were travelling without the aid of sirens, only because the main road was quiet at this time of the day.

Claire rang during the journey to confirm that the farm had been left to Ian Walcott and his son, Adam. She also informed them that Ian Walcott owned a Ford Transit van.

"That's it, up ahead on the right," Bob eagerly pointed out the entrance to the farm. There were a couple of barns at the front of the drive, and the farmhouse was tucked behind them. "The barns should provide us with enough cover to sneak up to the house."

"I was thinking the same," Sam agreed. She drew the car to a halt, and the other three cars in the convoy all stopped behind her.

The officers exited their vehicles and joined Sam, Bob and Suzanna on the pavement about fifty feet from the entrance to the farmyard.

"Okay, have any of you officers got Tasers?" Sam asked the uniformed men.

"Two of us, Dale and myself."

"That makes four of us. In that case, we'll take the lead. Suzanna, if it all kicks off in there, I'd prefer it if you waited until the dust settles before you join us."

"Fair enough, boss."

Sam and Oliver took the lead with Dale and Paul right behind them and Bob, Liam and Alex bringing up the rear. Sam scanned every direction once they entered the farmyard. She dashed off to the left with the others close behind her. She crept to the end of the barn to observe the farmhouse that appeared to be in need of either demolishing or a major renovation. Either way, it seemed a strange location to hold the kids captive.

"I can see someone standing by the downstairs window at the front, possibly on the lookout; just be aware of that as we get closer," Sam said.

A couple of the men passed the message to the rest of the team.

"Oliver, get ready to go. We'll head for the back door. Dale and Paul, you can cover us. Keep out of sight with an eye trained on the front of the house."

Sam moved out, crouching low. She darted across the farmyard to the rear of the property but stopped close to the edge of the building, ensuring neither of the criminals was in the back garden. With the coast clear, she gestured to Oliver that it was time to make their move. Dale and Paul ran after them but stopped at the side of the farmhouse, allowing themselves to keep an eye on the front.

"Let's get in there. I'm not one for hanging around. There's only one vehicle outside, the van we've been searching for. I'm taking a punt they're alone in the house. Well, the father and son and hopefully the three kids. My idea is to hit them fast and hard, not giving them the time to gain access to the kids, if they're locked away in a separate room somewhere."

"Sounds good to me," Oliver agreed.

Sam counted down with her fingers, three, two, one, and then entered the rear garden. She tried the handle on the back door and, to her surprise and relief, it opened. "Get your Taser ready. I'm not going to hang around. As soon as we see one of them, we give them the option to surrender then fire if they fail to do it."

Oliver nodded, and Sam pushed open the back door. She paused to listen. Somewhere in the near distance, voices, but she wasn't sure if it was from the TV or whether the father and son were having a conversation. She crept across to the doorway that led into the hallway and paused to listen again. It didn't take Sam long to work out the voices were coming from the room next door to the kitchen. She aimed her Taser at the doorway and carried out another countdown on her fingers, then she and Oliver made their move.

"Hands in the air. Do it!" she shouted as they ran into the room.

What she saw horrified her. Two men were overseeing three small boys dissecting animals on the dining table on the other side of the room.

The men glanced up and seemed stunned to see them standing there.

Sam stared at the boys, and seeing the enjoyment on the three angelic faces sickened her. Turning her attention back to the men, she ordered, "Step away from the children, slowly. I'll give you to the count of three to do as I say." She was conscious the kids were still holding the knives, although she couldn't see the men had any weapons in their hands.

"Ahh, here she is. We've been expecting you, Inspector. What took you so long to find us?" The older man laughed.

Her gaze met his, and her stomach turned over. "Did you harm Rhys, Ian Walcott?"

He smiled. "Sadly not, that stroke of genius was all down to my son here. I've trained him well over the last six months."

"Obviously not well enough because you've both been caught," she retorted and grinned.

"Ah, but what fun we've had along the way." He ducked quickly and grasped something from beside the sofa—it was a gun.

However, Sam's quick-thinking prevented him from using it. She fired her Taser, and fifty thousand volts hit his body. He dropped to the floor before he realised what was happening.

"Go on, make my day," Oliver warned Adam as he attempted to move towards them, hatred and intent filling his young eyes.

"Fucking police, you're all a waste of space." His attention turned back to the kids, and he raised his arm to hook it around the nearest boy's throat, but Oliver read the situation well and fired his Taser.

Sam released her finger on the trigger and ran to open the front door. "It's all clear," she shouted and then rushed back to the lounge.

Oliver released his finger, and both criminals remained where they were as the room flooded with their colleagues.

While the male officers dealt with the Walcotts, Suzanna

and Sam checked the kids were all right and removed the knives from their hands. In the melee that followed, Bob was the first to suggest Social Services should be contacted and placed the call.

The Walcotts were helped to their feet. Both men resisted arrest and tried to reach for the children, but Sam and Suzanna blocked their way.

"You haven't heard the last of this," Ian warned.

"As serial killers go, you were sloppy, accept it," Sam goaded him. "Get them out of my sight."

He shouted expletives all the way through the house. Once the noise quietened down, Sam ran upstairs and pulled a sheet off one of the beds. She entered the lounge again, asked the boys to step away from the table and covered the dissected animals with the cloth.

"Are you okay, boys?"

The three of them huddled together, scared witless. Sam couldn't understand their reactions because they seemed to be enjoying themselves when she and Oliver had burst into the room.

None of the boys responded to her question. She encouraged them to sit on the sofa. Reluctantly, they slid past her and Suzanna and threw themselves on the threadbare two-seater.

Sam couldn't say what she wanted to say to Suzanna, not in front of the kids, but she was too scared to leave them alone while she held a conversation with her colleague out of earshot. Bob and Alex entered the lounge.

"Watch the kids for us, I need to have a chat with Suzanna outside."

Sam left the house and inhaled the clean fresh air, ridding herself of the smell of blood tainting her nostrils. "I just wanted to get your take on what went on in there."

"Are you talking about the boys' reactions?"

"Yes, did they seem off to you?"

Suzanna sighed. "Unfortunately, yes. I'm reluctant to admit this but I'm getting the impression the quicker they receive counselling the better, if that's available at their age."

Sam puffed out her cheeks as she thought. "I think you're right. Not only were they subjected to probably witnessing their mothers kill themselves, in the case of the first two kids who were abducted, but when we raided this place to find them dissecting rats and birds. I hate to say this, but they appeared to be enjoying the activity, too."

"It's not something a child of that age should have witnessed."

"We'll see what Social Services have to say when they arrive, they shouldn't be long now. What a shit show. I couldn't believe my bloody eyes when I walked in and saw that macabre scene, it took everything I had not to vomit."

"I wonder what the Walcotts' plans were for the boys. How soon they would have expected them to perfect their skills, not on other animals, but on a human being."

Sam raised her hand and shook her head. "Don't even go there. I suppose we have to be thankful we found them before any real damage was caused."

"They can't be alone in their way of thinking, the Walcotts, can they? What if there are other serial killers out there doing the exact same thing, recruiting boys of this age or slightly older, teaching them how to become serial killers?"

"Shit, don't. I really don't want to even contemplate that possibility, Suzanna."

"During the interview, it might be worth asking if there's a club they belong to, if only to gauge their reaction."

"You're right, I'll do that."

. . .

SOCIAL SERVICES eventually showed up at the farm an hour later. Sam and her team returned to the station to process the Walcotts. Sam was eager to get on with the interviews after they'd discussed the events of the day over a much-deserved cup of coffee.

"I think we'll tackle them at the same time. Alex and Oliver, do you want to conduct the interview with the son? While Bob and I see what Ian Walcott has to say for himself, if anything."

Alex smiled. "It would be a pleasure."

"Don't forget to raise the question about them possibly being members of a club, like Suzanna suggested, if only to gauge Adam's reaction."

"We'll do that, boss."

The four of them headed down the stairs to the interview rooms. A duty solicitor was already in attendance in each room. The Walcotts were escorted from their cells, two minutes apart.

Bob said the necessary verbiage for the recording, and Sam started bombarding Ian Walcott with questions. Walcott sat there, with a smug look, and predictably went down the 'no comment' route.

Sam ended the interview quickly and thanked the solicitor for attending, then she crossed the hallway to join Alex and Oliver to see if they were faring any better. Unfortunately, they had the same outcome with the son.

"Okay let's wind things up in here." She left the room and ventured upstairs to bring the rest of the team up to date. "We'll gather the evidence together. They won't be able to squirm their way out of this one, they were caught red-handed with the abducted children on site and literally, with blood on their hands. We've also got a star witness on board, Odell, who can give us a formal identification. Which reminds me, I need to give her a call as well as the other relatives, let them know the Walcotts have been caught."

"Why don't I do that?" Bob suggested. "Well, most of it. You could visit the hospital, tell Odell in person and fit in a visit with Rhys while you're there."

Sam smiled. "I like that idea, partner. If you're sure, I know you try to avoid dealing with the relatives when possible."

"It's about time I took on more responsibility, isn't that what you're always hinting at? Well, now is as good a time as any. Off you pop."

Sam saluted him and sniggered. "If that's an order, I'm out of here. Thanks for all your hard work, team. You never cease to amaze me."

EPILOGUE

Sam entered Odell's room; the woman was resting and stirred when she sensed Sam had arrived.

"Hello, Inspector. Do you have some news for me?"

"I think you'll find it's the best news ever. Damien has been found, safe and sound. He's being assessed by Social Services."

Odell closed her eyes and released the breath she'd been holding in. "Thank God. I genuinely thought I was never going to see him again. And the men who... did this to me and kidnapped my son?"

"They've been arrested. Don't worry, they'll get the punishment they deserve, and the other families will all get the justice they're seeking, as well."

Odell lifted her hand to shake Sam's. "I'll never be able to thank you enough for what you've done for me and my son."

"My team and I pulled out all the stops; we couldn't have done that without the information you gave us. The criminals dropped a clanger, they know that now."

"Leaving me alive?"

"Yes, all you need to do now is concentrate on your recovery, knowing that Damien is in safe hands at last."

"I'll do that." She rested her head against the pillow, and Sam crept out of the room.

When she poked her head around the door to Rhys' room, he was sitting upright, fully awake and alert. "Hey, you're looking so much better. How are you feeling?"

"You're right, I am. It's great seeing you, I've missed you heaps. Have you finished early today?"

"There was someone else I needed to visit at the hospital. Bob insisted I finish early, leaving him to wrap up everything back at the station."

"Wrap up? As in your investigation?"

"That's right. We've succeeded in solving four investigations this week, including yours."

He frowned. "What? You've caught the person who attacked me?"

"Yep, we figured out all four cases were connected." She kissed him lightly on the lips and sat on the edge of the bed, holding his hand while she ran through the events of the past few days.

"So, they came after me because I'm linked to you, is that what you're telling me?"

Sam cringed. "We believe so, although the father admitted that his son was the one who attacked you. Both men went down the 'no comment' route during the interviews. I'm sorry, love."

"What for? It was my decision to get involved with you. I knew what the risks were."

"Yes, but neither of us anticipated you getting hurt like this. I'll have to live with that guilt on my conscience for the rest of my life."

"Don't be ridiculous, Sam. We all have to take chances in

this life. Each day I share with you outweighs the risks a hundred to one."

"Bless you. I've been so concerned since I found that note…"

He inclined his head. "What note? Am I missing something?"

"One of the killers visited your room, not long after your operation, and left a note under your body. As soon as I discovered it, I rang my DCI. He insisted that an officer should be on duty outside your room twenty-four-seven."

"Ah, it's all making sense now. Jesus, did they do anything else to me?"

"No, I think their aim was to toy with us, keep us on our toes. They slipped up in the end, which led us to their location."

"Thank God for that."

He fell silent, and Sam could imagine the cogs turning in his mind.

"Hey, it's all good, there's no need for you to worry now," she reassured him.

"I'm not." He leaned over and removed something from his bedside drawer. He took her hand in his and said, "Sam Cobbs, we've been to hell and back over the last week, and it's made me realise that I would find it impossible to live without you. Will you marry me?" He placed a ring made of paper on the tip of her ring finger as he awaited her response.

Flabbergasted, tears misted her vision. "I'd be honoured."

They shared a kiss that she sensed would seal their future together.

THE END

. . .

Thank you for reading To Judge Them, the next thrilling adventure is To Fear Him

Have you read any of my other fast paced crime thrillers yet? Why not try the first book in the DI Sara Ramsey series No Right to Kill

Or grab the first book in the bestselling, award-winning, Justice series here, Cruel Justice.

Or the first book in the spin-off Justice Again series, Gone In Seconds.

Perhaps you'd prefer to try one of my other police procedural series, the DI Kayli Bright series which begins with The Missing Children.

Or maybe you'd enjoy the DI Sally Parker series set in Norfolk, Wrong Place.

Or my gritty police procedural starring DI Nelson set in Manchester, Torn Apart.

Or maybe you'd like to try one of my successful

psychological thrillers She's Gone, I KNOW THE TRUTH or Shattered Lives.

KEEP IN TOUCH WITH M A COMLEY

Pick up a FREE novella by signing up to my newsletter today.
https://BookHip.com/WBRTGW

BookBub
www.bookbub.com/authors/m-a-comley

Blog

http://melcomley.blogspot.com

Why not join my special Facebook group to take part in monthly giveaways.

Readers' Group

Printed in Dunstable, United Kingdom